BACKBONE

Short Stories by CAROL BLY

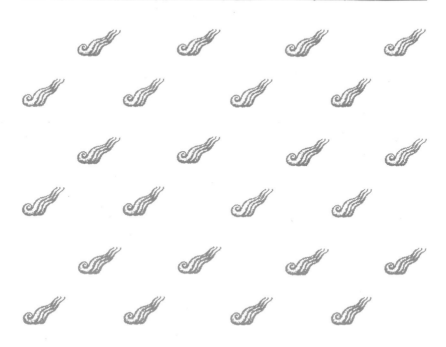

BACKBONE

Short Stories

by

CAROL BLY

1985
MILKWEED EDITIONS
MINNEAPOLIS, MINNESOTA

BACKBONE
Stories by Carol Bly

Published by Milkweed Editions
430 First Avenue North, Suite 400
Minneapolis, Minnesota 55401
Books may be ordered from the above address
Manufactured in the United States of America

Library of Congress Catalog Card Number: 84-61733
ISBN 0-915943-36-0

Backbone is the first of a Milkweed Editions Fiction
Series. This book is published with the aid of grant
support from *B Dalton*
BOOKSELLER

Fiction Series Editor: Emilie Buchwald
Fiction Series Designer: R.W. Scholes

Acknowledgments

These stories have appeared in the following magazines and anthologies.
They are reprinted by permission of the author and the respective
publishers: "The Last of the Gold Star Mothers." *The New Yorker.*
Copyright © 1979; "The Mouse Roulette Wheel." First published as
"Brothers" in *25 Minnesota Writers.* Copyright © 1980. Nodin Press, Inc.;
"The Dignity of Life." First published in *Ploughshares.* Reprinted in
The Best American Short Stories 1983. Houghton Mifflin Company;
"Talk of Heroes;" *Twin Cities Magazine.* Copyright © 1982; "Gunnar's
Sword." First published in *American Review.* Reprinted in *The Minne-
sota Experience. An Anthology of Minnesota Prose.* Copyright © 1979.
The Adams Press.

to Donald Hall

EDITOR'S PREFACE

Carol Bly is a storyteller, in the best old-fashioned sense of that word. As a storyteller, she speaks in a voice capable of great emotional range, informed by a wit that is wickedly on-target. She is a powerful observer of emotional chill.

Bly has written: "The principle of literature is devotion to the particulars of life. Chekhov, for example, is not particularly universal; he is particularly particular." The stories in *Backbone* are filled with particulars —Mary Graving's woodworking tools in a basement once devoted to home canning and laundry tubs, the Showing Room in Jack Canon's funeral parlor, the fair isle knitting and braided rugs in the craft room at the Jacob Lutheran Home— all a part of the rich weave of Bly's stories. Bly makes us intimately at home in the places her characters live. We know the rooms they work in and the routes they drive to get where they're going. We get plastered with them at the Rachel River V.F.W., and stop for coffee at the Feral Café in St. Aiden. It is as good as or better than eavesdropping because we get to follow people around and see whether their words accord with their thoughts— which we, but not those others, in the story, are privileged to know.

The stories remind us that, in fact, words don't necessarily mirror thoughts; that we don't usually say what we mean, nor do we usually mean quite what we say. Bly focuses our attention on the gulf between what is thought and felt and what is actually said. The vestrymen in the opening scene of "The Mouse Roulette Wheel" despise one another. We hear what they *would* say to one another if civilized convention failed them, but they are not "brave or crazy" enough to speak what they truly feel. Instead, they must maintain a false cheerfulness and companionableness. Since they can't hack each other to bits conversationally, they manage to have a good time by sharing stories about the deaths of others, the "especially grisly deaths." Bly's prose catches this conspiratorial sublimation perfectly: "The little circle of men drew in; their voices sagged joyfully."

As we read, we learn that the lakes and woods and fields of the Minnesota landscape are not so serene and undisturbed as they appear; the subterranean realities are the gated lakes ready to be tapped for needy cities, the corporation maps showing the platts for future strip mining, the failed dairy farms bought up for real estate development, Pine County staked out for uranium prospecting. The earth's capital is up for grabs, for quick money or money to be carefully invested.

When Father Bill Hewlitt tells the cook to make generous hamburgers for the St. Matthew's Episcopal church bazaar, she snaps back immediately: "What about the money?" Money, the lack of it, and the desire for it, percolates through the strata of these stories, linked to the issue of cost as opposed to actual value. In "The Last of the Gold Star Mothers," Mary Graving takes pleasure in making the beautiful, sturdy toys which form an important part of her income. A well-to-do businessman, a childhood friend who recognizes the quality of her goods, tries to cheat her in a business arrangement—this, although he knows her circumstances. There are also those who accept the world's pricetag for everything: Francis Hewlitt, Father Bill's brother, cannot understand why his family won't accept the money he wants to leave them.

Jack Canon, who has a lifetime's practice in not saying what he thinks or showing what he feels, lives in a state of emotional numbness which may help to account for his installation of the Casket Lighting Plan, Bly's marvelous, Swiftian jab at human mendacity. Thus, Canon astounds himself when he shouts at Molly Galan what he's really thinking. Only the strong stimulus of many conflicting emotions allows him to override his self-damning reserve.

The people in these stories long for these moments when the spirit cries out and gets fed. Sometimes it is no more than a glance keenly felt, or a few words, like Willi Varig's to Emily Anderson when they meet after twenty-five years in "Talk of Heroes." But sometimes it is the ecstasy Harriet White feels holding a baby in her arms again.

From the perspective of the media values of American culture, these characters are over the hill, all washed up, out of it; they are unfashionably middle-aged or just plain old. Mary Graving is in her thirties, Father Bill Hewlitt is forty-one, Emily Anderson is in her fifties, Jack Canon is sixty-three and Harriet White —who must be one of the most inspiriting heroines in contemporary fiction— is eighty-two. According to our cultural suppositions, these people, with the possible exception of Mary Graving, are no longer having significant emotional experiences; they ought to be content just to get out to buy their groceries. But here we recognize what should not be a surprise; that we never lose the need and the desire to touch and be touched by other life; that passion, physical and spiritual, does not die until we do, though it may be forced underground.

The final paragraph of "Gunnar's Sword" is elegant, subtly knit, emotionally resonant—one of many such passages. But the most characteristic feature of this prose is that it moves with the freedom and muscle of vigorous speech, the vigorous speech we come to expect from the characters.

Their voices, distinctive and determined, ask questions and give their views of what it's all about: "Uniquely filthy" is sheriff LeRoy Beske's summing up of American and European culture. Spiteful, greedy Estona Huutula, querulous LaVonne Morstad, the suavely brutal Gestapo officer who interrogates Willi Varig, and even Lorraine Mosely whom we only hear for a moment on the telephone—each is vivid. Bly has a delicate ear for the way people talk; she gives them free rein to be funny (and they often are), and to reflect upon themselves. They are not excused; neither are they made pitiable or caricatured.

The fragile spine that lets us bend also allows us to stand. Carol Bly celebrates the valor it takes to live humanely.

Emilie Buchwald

CONTENTS

The Last of the Gold Star Mothers

ON A WINDLESS EARLY EVENING in October, almost the best time of day of the best time of year in Minnesota, no one was standing on the escarpment path in Rachel River County Park, where you can look out over the fir forests toward Lake Superior and the distant glow of lights of West Duluth. The park was deserted, in fact—no one was leaning on the old W.P.A.-built wall to watch the Rachel River falling perfectly from one black stone to the next, eventually to find its way down the escarpment to the place where it joins the St. Louis River. People in Rachel River keep busy, and sometimes they seem too distracted to see things. No one, for instance, had noticed a battered safe, which sat in the bed of the stream in the park. It had been stolen from a Union 76 gas station a month earlier, in a celebrated local crime. The thief had been found out and caught, but the safe, torch-cut open and dumped right in the middle of Rachel River, still lay among the rocks, and the slight, spindly water fell on it without variance.

On this particular evening, a Tuesday, most of the regular people—that is, not the Duluth Airbase personnel and their wives, who don't count, but the *regulars*—were down at the Rachel River V.F.W. Lounge. Drinks, for once, were at half price, in honor of Mr. and Mrs. Kevin Ohlaug's son, Curt. Everyone explained to everyone else that Curt Ohlaug had been in the service in some native place called Engola or Angola, no one knew in what branch of the service, but, anyway, now he was back, and drinks were at half price. The local radio-news lady, a thirty-three-year-old divorcée named Mary Graving, sat in the best corner booth of the V.F.W. Lounge. She was celebrating something secretly. From the beginning, she had intended to spend the whole evening there, so she had had the foresight to prop herself up in the right angle between the back of the booth and the wall. By her elbow, someone had scratched on the wall a suggestion to the I.R.S. about what it could do with itself. Mary had arranged a smile on her face quite a while ago; now it was safely fixed there, and she herself was safely fixed, and although she was immensely drunk, she was not so drunk as the others, which meant she counted as dead sober.

When Mary Graving was sober, her face was too decided and twitchy to look good with the large plain earrings she always wore. She thought she was generally too grim-looking, and her earrings looked too cheerful at the edges of her face. Now that she was drunk, though, and wearing a red dress, her face felt hot and rosy. Her smile stayed stuck on, and she knew that the earrings — a new pair, especially cheap, not from Bagley's in Duluth but a product of the Ben Franklin Store in Rachel River — looked fine. She was not beautiful but she was all right.

She was crowded into the booth with seven local people whose familiar faces were getting blurred. One was LeRoy Beske, the sheriff. Each person had a hand round his glass, and their fingers looked silvery in the night-club lighting. The fingers were numb and stiff with drink, as silvery and thick as fingers in the empty suits of armor in city museums. No one is shallow and vulgar forever; sooner or later the whole species likes to be profound. Now, after everyone had pleased everyone else by adding comments to the I.R.S. graffito, a moment came when LeRoy Beske was profound. The others could take it from him, the sheriff explained, that all of culture — all of American culture, and that went for the Europeans, too, they weren't any better — was getting more and more slovenly and cowardly and uniquely filthy. The sheriff repeated the last phrase clearly, as sonorous as John Donne. "Yes," he said, "uniquely filthy." In 1946 he had stood on the Boulevard Saint-Germain with his buddies, and he could assure them the French, too, like everyone else, even the French with their fancy Paris, were uniquely filthy. Everyone in the booth marvelled at every remark. A hundred philosophies brimmed wonderfully in their heads.

That was Tuesday night. At nine-thirty the next morning, Wednesday, the dispatcher's room in the Rachel River jail was softened by sunlight that slanted through the barred horizontal windows. Kristi Marie, who covered the radio, was filling out court forms at her desk under the two radio speakers; a deputy named DeWayne Sorkelson sat at another desk, idly making throws onto the blotter from a dice cup. The sheriff himself leaned by one of the windows, watching for the other deputy, Merle Schaefer, to come in. Everything was as usual, but the team was a little nervous this morning, because Kristi Marie and DeWayne knew that LeRoy Beske was going to put the scare onto Merle whenever he showed up. Now and then, while they waited, a message came crackling in on the radio; Kristi Marie replied, and a voice would say "Ten-four," and the radio went off again.

Kristi Marie was on the two-way for the forenoon, but she had told them plainly that someone else would have to cover in the afternoon, because she and five other girls were going in a car to Duluth, to an art gallery. A member of their study club had suggested that with the world getting the way it was in so many places, it was a shame to throw away the cultural opportunities they had, what with Rachel River being only eleven miles away from Duluth, so Kristi Marie was going. Now the sheriff straightened up. Merle had appeared outside the jail, where he paused on the concrete steps and gave a languid smile to a little boy named Gregsy Hanson, whose face shone up at him. Poor kid, the sheriff thought. Gregsy Hanson's dad sold him out for the bottle, and his mother sold out everybody in town. When she went down the aisles in the Super Valu she even sold out her baby as he sat in the cart, explaining his faults to everyone in the produce section. And now, the sheriff thought, even this cop that Gregsy admired wasn't much good. Merle came in the jailhouse door, and Gregsy stood one-legged on the concrete, with his other knee thrown over the seat of his bike, as he watched him go. The *Duluth Herald* bag lay, caved in, in his bike basket.

"Turn on the radio to KTRW, so we get the Rachel River program when it comes on," the sheriff said to Kristi Marie. "Turn it low until she comes on, though."

Merle came in, raising a hand to his glossy thick hair. He was having an affair with a woman named Verona McIvor, in Floodwood, and whenever he looked in the mirror of his cop car he saw a man involved with a woman, and with women generally—a gigantic man hopelessly wrapped in physical satisfactions, his own desires, women's desires for him. When he walked, there was a lunge about his walking, as if he carried several women on his shoulders, clinging; they clung all about him, and his walk supported the great weight of them.

"All right, Merle," the sheriff said.

He's going to bust me for seeing Verona, Merle thought, instantly noticing that no one in the room would look at him. I don't want no counterculture job selling auto parts to farmers, he thought.

I want this job. I want the uniform. His quick glance out the window showed him that that little kid, Gregsy Hanson, was still standing there waiting to look at him, Merle.

"O.K., Merle," the sheriff said. "We live in one lousy, slovenly time of United States history, but there is one lousy, slovenly thing that's not going to happen again in Rachel River County. O.K.? O.K. Labor Day you were in charge of the Gold Star Mothers' car in the parade, right? O.K., the parade forms in front of the Vision Avenue Apartments where you pick up the Gold Star Mother, the only one we got left, and then everyone marches and drives to the cemetery where they have the doings. I got two complaints on you. First, you stuffed our one remaining Gold Star Mother into the car so mean she got bruised. She brought a charge. But that isn't all. Then you got to the cemetery, and I suppose I ought to be grateful you didn't run down them Rachel River Saddle Club horses on the way. When you got to the cemetery, what'd you do but get out and turn off the ignition, which means the air-conditioning went off. You left the windows rolled up and you left the Gold Star Mother in there. Mrs. Lorraine Graving is not a young woman; it was a hundred and five Fahrenheit. She could have died in there. I would like you to know that she is a symbol of our whole national honor. Without her we wouldn't be the kind of country we are today. Now, if we're not going to have any respect any more, it'll be the end of the Gold Star Mother program completely."

Merle was so relieved it was not about this woman that he was seeing in Floodwood that he had to work to keep from smiling. He would not lose his job over stuffing a Gold Star Mother into a Ford.

He said, "Yes, sir," in a tone he had heard on a police program on TV.

"And there's another thing," the sheriff said. "You regard yourself as this big hand with the ladies."

"No, sir," Merle said with great dignity.

"Well, since you're such a great man with the ladies," the sheriff went on, "I've got something you can do today. You know her—it's Mrs. Blatke, that widow of that guy committed suicide. Well, I want you to find her, and then you make it clear to her she doesn't call the police anymore. I know she's upset. I know her husband robbed the Union 76 station and we caught him, and I know he killed himself. I took that refresher course on police psychology and I know she blames herself or something, but that don't mean

she can go round town getting in fights with everyone all over
Rachel River and then call the police. O.K.? And I don't want you
to tell her mean. Tell her nice but firm. And don't make a pass at
her."

"You got to be kidding!" Merle shouted. "Make a pass at Mrs.
Blatke! Listen, nobody would serve as a pallbearer at her husband's funeral, and who volunteers but me, and I got the five others,
too!"

"Yes," the sheriff said. "And then later that night you called her
up and word is you made a pass at her."

Kristi Marie waved one hand at them and turned up the volume
on the speakers. "And now," the radio announcer's voice said, "we
go to Mary Graving, in Rachel River, for the Rachel River County
news. Good morning, Mary!"

"Good morning, Bert!" said Mary. Her voice sounded a little
husky, because it was carried by telephone from her house at the
south end of Rachel River to the Duluth studio and then the eleven
miles back again by radio.

"Today is the Feast of St. Maurus," Mary said. She did not sound
very hung over.

"Gee, she's got a nice voice," the sheriff said. "I'm glad she took
that job, since she had to get a job. Is it true she's got nerves?"

"I don't know," Kristi Marie said. "I heard that, too. But she
always seems real cheerful." Kristi Marie tipped her plump face up
toward the loudspeaker over her desk. "She never forgets anything,
either," she added. "She had it on five times to remind people to
bring potluck to the St. John's annual meeting, and that's not even
her church, she didn't need to have." They all listened to the radio
over the quiet whine of the jail fan. The sheriff and the other officer
had begun casting the dice to see who paid afternoon coffee.

"Although today is actually the Feast of St. Maurus, we haven't
got any reliable information about his life, and for a very special
reason I'd like to tell you, instead, about St. Alban," the radio said.

"But she shouldn't have religion on the radio," Kristi Marie
said. "Last time they had religion on, we got seven phone calls
from Lutherans saying they didn't want that Catholic crap on the
radio, and nine calls from Catholics saying they wanted equal time
if they were going to have that kind of Lutheran crap on."

"Speaking of religion," the sheriff said. "Do you remember
when that occult group cut up all those cattle, over toward Perham?"

"I remember that," Kristi Marie said.

"It is too bad that St. Alban isn't better known," Mary was saying over the radio, "because we have a man in Rachel River with a
birthday today, who is here, alive, able to celebrate that birthday,
just because of people in France who did what St. Alban did long
before that. St. Alban was the first martyr in the British Isles. During some persecutions, Roman soldiers were going around pick-
ing up Christians to torture them, and a legionnaire came to
Alban's door and said, 'We are looking for a certain escaped Christian.' Well, this Christian was hiding in Alban's attic, and Alban
had traded clothes with him. 'Yes, I know,' Alban said. 'I am the
one you are looking for.' 'You don't look like him,' the soldier
said. Alban said, 'Look at my clothes—look at me. I'm the one you
want.' The Roman soldier was stubborn, however, and said,
'Somehow, you don't look like the right man.' But then he thought,
I've got to bring in somebody, and it is getting late, so finally he
said, 'All right, all right'—whatever the Latin or Celtic for 'All
right, all right' is—and he took in Alban, and they killed him.

"During World War Two," Mary's radio voice went on, "underground forces in Occupied Europe faced the same sort of thing Alban faced. It must have been terrifying to have someone knock at
night and explain he was an American flier or an underground intelligence agent, and could you hide him? You always knew that if
the Germans caught you, you would be tortured for information
and then likely killed. Well, Mahlon Hanson, of Rachel River,
who gets our radio birthday greetings today, is alive because somebody was brave enough to risk self and family to hide him, thirty-
four years ago, and help him reach the Channel. And, speaking of
help, what better help could you expect than to have your next
winter's furnace costs cut in half—that's right, cut right in half.
You couldn't do better than to plan now, because if fall is here,
winter can't be far behind, and Merv Skjolestad is carrying a line of
woodburning stoves that can make hundreds of dollars of savings
for *you*."

When the program was over, Mary replaced the telephone receiver in its cradle, turned off the power box, and unplugged the
cassette player she used for taping town-council notices. The Duluth station had set up this radio-telephone hookup for her in her
own basement. To Mary, the program meant a tiny, unfailing income, with the marvelous virtue that she could be home when her
children, Will and Molly, got home from school every day. The

other end of the basement was reserved for her toymaking business. Between the radio program and the toymaking, Mary spent many hours every day in the cool, brightly lighted basement. The old cellar shelves were soft and grainy with rot; the previous renter, an A.F.D.C. mother, had left loops of rusty Kerr-top canning rings there, but Mary had scrubbed off the space she needed, and spread out the tools of her trade there—a dish of chuck keys, a small sabre saw, two sizes of nail sets, all her lacquers, a mitre box, her power saws and sander. The place reminded one that generations of women had stored home canning there and had filled and emptied laundry tubs into the sump hole; there was an aura of domestic bravery and domestic squalor about the place still. But now the basement had some glint and bustle, too, which came from Mary's shiny, imposingly modern radio equipment on the desk, her squared-off drawings on the steel table, and the bright-orange electrical drop cords curling everywhere. In the middle of the room, and in the space where a washing machine had been before the men had recently come and repossessed it, there stood several half-finished castles and Norman keeps and three-storeyed doll houses, all smelling beautifully of AC ply.

On school-day afternoons, the children would burst into the house above her; the old farmhouse shuddered when they struck the door with their knuckles and books. Mary would climb the basement stairs dazedly, and in the shabby living room she and Will and Molly would drink cocoa, sitting in front of a print of two sailing ships over the mantel. The ships were heavily square-rigged. They tore along in the lunging, green, tremendously deep Atlantic. The children loved to say, "Just think what would happen if a man fell overboard into the sea!" And Mary usually assured them solemnly, "It must have been nearly impossible, in those days, to put her about to pick up anyone." Sometimes Mary explained as much about the rigging as she understood. They all drank their cocoa and speculated silently about a man overboard treading water in the deep sea and watching his ship grow smaller as it sailed away and left him. Then, on most days, the children went outdoors to play, and Mary went into the kitchen. Little by little, the hours of silent work in the basement would sift from her mind, until soon her supper-making seemed perfectly practical, perfectly pleasant, in the way that hobbies are pleasant when you get your mind off your life work. If they were having pastry for dinner, she gave it her attention and got it right.

But just now, in October, Will and Molly were spending a week at Pike Lake with their father, Cordell. As Mary worked on a bookcase she was building as a surprise for them, she kept track of the quarter hours as she waited for the time, arranged with Cordell, when she would telephone and talk to them. The calling hour was agreed on for midday on Wednesday, since school would be closed then for a Teachers' In-Service. Across from where Mary sat, there stood the old, red-painted steel table, on which she kept her drawings of toys and her general accounts. In her childhood, in Duluth, there had been metal furniture in two places in her house— in the maids' room in the basement and out on the shaded, north-facing terrace. Every spring, the terrace furniture was repainted by the hired man and then set out on the stone flagging. All summer, it never seemed to lose its chill. Mary had been expected to take part in her mother's teas out there, when she had to listen to her mother's friends and their little quarrels about books. They sat on the painted metal in their silk dresses, and responded to one another in flurries. "Oh, but Julia," they cried, "can you really say that with impunity?" Mary sometimes found herself staring down, past the terrace ferns, into the window of the maids' room in the basement. She could see the two iron beds there. Her own basement, Mary sometimes felt now, was not unlike the maids' room.

Sitting by the unfinished bookcase, Mary fitted new paper into her sander. At the same time, she was estimating her income for the current year. The bookcase was to have a lever on one side, which opened a secret vertical shaft that would run from the top to the bottom of the case, at its back. On the opposite side, the left, there would be a fishing reel fastened to the case, which was to operate a miniature dumbwaiter inside the secret shaft. She meant to make a tiny velvet-covered chest to fit in the dumbwaiter, in which the children could keep their treasures—whatever they liked. She was not building this bookcase to be sold, and for this reason her face was mobile, nervous, and sometimes smiling as she worked. Her facial tic was not so bad as it was sometimes. The other toys standing about—the apartment-building doll houses, the sixteenth-century half-timbered dollhouses, the castles, and the puppet show—were all parts of her business. They sold at prices from sixty-five dollars to four hundred dollars each.

Before she became self-supporting, she had never imagined that one tends to do major economic calculations over and over again in one's head, as if the figures might improve with repetition. She knew that her total intake this past year would be eleven thousand three hundred dollars, but she kept refiguring it. Now she added things up again while she carefully drilled a hole for the fishing-reel cable to run through. The twenty-minute radio program, five days a week, brought her five hundred dollars a month, which was six thousand dollars a year. If she got orders for four large castles at three hundred and fifty dollars each, that would be fourteen hundred dollars, which made a total so far of seventy-four hundred. Ten medium-sized castles would bring in fifteen hundred dollars more, making a total of eight thousand nine hundred. In the first year after he had left her, Cordell sent her eleven out of the twelve agreed-upon monthly child-support payments; in the second year, he sent ten. Now she figured he would send an average of, say, eight payments per year for another year or so. At one hundred and fifty dollars per child, that brought the total to eleven thousand three hundred dollars. It was not really enough.

She worked at the children's bookcase for an hour, getting used to the pleasure and irritations of the task. She liked to work fast, watching her hands touching things gently. She disliked her habit of sometimes carrying a pencil or nails in her mouth. Presently, she went over to the radio table and telephoned a farm-equipment dealer named Merv Skjolestad to suggest that she write him an ad for his Patz manure-movers, which she could alternate with the ads she now read over the radio for his Schweiss woodburning furnace. She could alternate the ads—Monday-Wednesday-Friday and Tuesday-Thursday. Merv told her that wasn't all he had. He had a whole new line of grain-storage bins and some brand new milk-house equipment. She took down the sizes and prices, and told him she could do the furnaces on Mondays, the grain and milk-house line Tuesdays, and the Patz equipment and furnaces by turn on Wednesdays, Thursdays, and Fridays. She eased him off the telephone in time to call the children at the prearranged time.

She listened to the telephone ring twenty times. Then she decided she might have misdialled, so she called again and let it ring ten more times. After a while, she went upstairs to wash her face, which looked awful. She was a person whose eyes puffed up quickly.

She gathered her sheets and clothes from a basket and drove to the other end of town, to the laundromat. She was very sorry to find a woman she knew named Mrs. Blatke in the laundromat, sorting through a pile of unclaimed clothing. "Why, hello," said Mrs. Blatke, in a false tone. Mrs. Blatke's voice was not perfectly respectful, because although her husband had been caught knocking over the Union 76 station and then had felt so bad that he couldn't support her and their kids that he had committed suicide, at least he had been a faithful husband to her, and this Mrs. Mary Graving might be a big shot, with a big-shot job running the radio program from Rachel River and selling fancy toys to big shots in Duluth, but the fact was Mrs. Blatke's husband had died and Mrs. Graving's husband had just up and left her. Mrs. Blatke, therefore, did not move over enough to let Mary Graving get her laundry bag between the folding table and the line of machines. Mary, on her side, knew that Mrs. Blatke stole clothing from people's dryer loads if they were not watching, so she did not say "Excuse me," when her laundry bag hit Mrs. Blatke's leg, with the sharp edge of the Cheer box inside the bag doing the hitting. Then Mary thought of something she must have forgotten in her car, and she went back out and came back in and squeezed by Mrs. Blatke again and hit her legs all over again.

"Funny a lady like you having to use the laundromat," Mrs. Blatke said after a while. "I've heard if you miss one payment on a washing machine they will repossess it, these days. But I wouldn't know. I was never one to buy stuff I couldn't afford and then have to have it repossessed."

Mary looked thoughtfully out the window. "I doubt if that cop is coming to look for me," she said aloud. "I never have had cops coming after me in a laundromat. Maybe he's got something to say just to you? I could step outside."

Mrs. Blatke jerked around and peered out the steamed window. "That's a no-good cop," she said warmly.

"He isn't much," Mary said.

They gave each other a quick look and then Mrs. Blatke said, actually in a kindly tone, "He did volunteer to be a pallbearer at my poor hubby's funeral, though, and no one else would, because . . . because."

"I know," Mary said. "And I'm sorry about your husband, too."

Outside, in the autumn sunshine, the policeman leaned against his car, idly smoothing his glossy black hair.

Mary didn't wait to dry her clothes, but took them wet from the machine and got into her car and drove away from the laundromat.

In the rearview mirror, she saw the policeman—whose name she now remembered: Merle—amble into the building.

She had an appointment with a man named Fran Paddock for three o'clock at Ye Olde 61—a kind of roadhouse dinner club, which he and a partner, who did some sort of cooking for the place, had recently bought. Now they were going to keep it open in the afternoons, too, in order to sell quality tourist items. The club stood halfway between Pike Lake and Rachel River, on a bypassed highway that supported a sprinkling of businesses that had been thrown up in the last few years where there had once been endless jack-pine forest. There were still patches of forest here and there, but as one drove along one saw the high domes of oil-storage tanks among the trees, and sometimes whole vistas of new, barracklike housing opened out. There was a turmoil about the landscape, as if it might all turn into a single giant shopping center by morning.

Mary walked into the orange, varnished-log building. In the dining room there was one table, over by the window, that didn't have chairs placed on top of it. A youngish man with sandy hair came out of the kitchen, opening his palms in an apologetic gesture.

"I'm Fran's partner," he said. "I can't shake hands, I'm baking—but at least I set up some place for you two to sit."

They both looked out the window next to the table. "I'm feeding bears out there," he said. "This time of year, sometimes three or four come lumbering up."

"Bears-shmears!" a cheerful voice said behind them.

It was Fran. Long ago, he and Mary had gone to school together in Duluth. Looking at him now, in the shadowy restaurant, Mary could see that he had changed less than she had in the past fifteen years. He still had the undeniably comely looks and extroverted expression that had never caught her interest when she was a girl. The basis of their friendship was not their few dances together at the Northland Country Club in the summers but their nerveless and violently competitive dinghy racing at the Duluth Yacht Club, on Lake Superior. They had both won a lot of races, and Fran had probably beaten her a few more times than she had beaten him; the Coast Guard had had to bring them in out of trouble more times than all the other Duluth sailors put together.

"I see you've introduced yourselves," Fran said now with his old grace. "Mary's an old friend—and a great sailor, too."

He sat down; Mary sat down. Fran's partner hovered for a moment, and he and Mary exchanged a glance. They hadn't introduced themselves at all, and now Fran was still talking about sailing in the old days. Mary understood that he was probably being extra gregarious in order to assure her that even if they were meeting on business he did not discount his old association with her. He was trying to lessen the tension of one person being there to sell the other one something—telling her that he knew she was not trading in on old acquaintance for commercial use—or that if she was, he was not offended.

"I still say there's nowhere you get that sense of reality that you do sailing," he said. "Hiked way out over the side—close to the water like that—you're touching down on reality. . . . But why should I tell that to you, of all people?"

"I haven't sailed in years now," Mary said with a smile.

She noticed that Fran immediately looked away when she said this, the way rich people sometimes do when they are afraid that a friend is about to explain that he has had to retrench.

Fran's partner wandered back into his kitchen, and Mary and Fran began to talk business. From time to time, as they discussed orders and discounts, she heard the baker slapping dough in the kitchen.

"There won't be any plastics," Fran said. "Strictly good things. What we're dealing with here is the guilty father. The children have been with him all weekend, say, and now it's Sunday afternoon, late, and they've been cross and that made *him* cross and he got sharp with them, but he doesn't want to deliver them back to their mother with them remembering that, so he stops in at Ye Olde 61, and buys them these very good toys. It'll work, Mary. When the kids get home, the mother turns over the toys, looking at the labels, checking to see if they're just strictly Airport, but Ye Olde 61 toys won't be Airport—so Dad will end up way ahead. O.K.! Let's see what you have, Mary. One of my real resources is what you are."

She showed him drawings and descriptions and Polaroid pictures of her work. She saw he could tell that the things she had made were really first class—especially the French townhouse, with its blue-green mansard roof and the tiny sign painted on the smudgy cream outside wall: "Défense d'Afficher par la Loi de 1881."

Fran laughed. "We need a tiny wooden toy dog out there peeing on that lamppost," he said. "It would be a great selling point. The

French are great on peeing."

The moment Fran said this, Mary knew he was going to cheat her clean. In the next few minutes, he did make an unfair consignment offer for her major toys, and said he would not handle the small ones. "What you really need are stuffed animals made with art fabrics," he said. "Or, you know—that quilted sculpture. Can you come up with a line of that?"

"Kids hate those art toys," Mary said.

"Yes, but they're very counterculture-looking, and that's in," Fran said.

He glanced out the window. "Hey, one of your bears has come in!" he shouted toward the kitchen.

The baker hurried in and bent over their table to look out the window. His arms, sanded all over with whole-wheat flour, were very near Mary's face. Mary and Fran and the baker watched a huge bear moving things around outside, lifting garbage, studying it.

"They're like dancers, compared to how dogs move," offered the baker.

After a while, Mary got up. "I'll get back to you on the consignments," she said to Fran.

"Remember, Mary," he said. "This is big. The guilty fathers, the classy toys, the grimy, whining kids *wanting* something. And don't forget to glue a dog onto the French apartment-building one. And how about a trademark, like *La Vraie Chose*. That could be your mark, Mary—*La Vraie Chose* on all your toys. It's a terrific idea!"

She smiled. He wasn't mistaken. It was a sound idea; his shop was a sound idea. As she drove home, she felt so low-spirited that she forgot she was secretly celebrating, last night and today, and was not going to be sad.

Back in Rachel River, she had one more appointment. She drove to the Vision Avenue Senior Citizen Apartments, where Mr. Dahle, the manager, said it was nice of her to come on time because it made him just so nervous when people weren't punctual. He expected punctuality of himself, he said; he expected it of others. "The problem is Lorraine, your mother-in-law," he said. "Or should I still call her your mother-in-law?"

"I guess she still is my mother-in-law," Mary told him.

"It's been five months since the rent was paid," Mr. Dahle said, holding his palms upward. "Now, I have discussed with Mrs. Graving—Lorraine—would she go on welfare. That is a practical

move, you know, and there is no disgrace to it. She told me her son
Cordell would pay the rent. I said, 'Well, he hasn't paid it for five
months now.' Then she said I was lying and trying to cheat an old
woman out of the rent, and she would call Cordell and he would
drive over from Pike Lake and show me a thing or two. So I said,
'Well, you might as well call him, because if he comes in I can ask
him in person will he pay the rent or not.' Then she grabs her Gold
Star flag off the window and shakes it at me and says, 'You see this
Gold Star? If you treat me wrong there's a lot of people who are
going to remember what this stands for, and they won't like it.' I
told her I am not treating her wrong, I am trying to get the rent
paid is all."

"I'll go up," Mary said.

Her mother-in-law, Lorraine Graving, was crouched by the
window, lifting the Gold Star flag up so she could see out. She was
stooped but full of spring. "Ooh, did you see that!" the old lady
said. "My, but there's a fight going on down there! Look at that—
that grown woman grabbed that boy's bike and threw it right
down on the sidewalk! Crazy! And she's left her car parked right
out in the middle of the street!"

She turned and looked at Mary. "*Ja*, I know why you're here,"
she said. "Now, you listen to me. I'm not letting that Dahle push
me around, and I'm not going to let *you* push me around. You
never gave Cordell the least bit of love and support. I always helped
him and he always said, 'Mama, I'm going to take care of you when
you're old.' Well, now I'm old and he is taking care of me. He was
always an affectionate boy, Cordell was. I can't say the same for his
brother Emmitt. Emmitt's the boy I lost. I don't suppose you ever
met Emmitt. During the war, you know how people went around
showing you all the letters they got from their sons, with those
A.P.O. numbers, and *reading* you the letters, too? Well, we never
got any from Emmitt—not a one. He seemed to be just as glad to be
away from home. We was running forty head of cattle in those
days, and they never took both boys off a farm. One would get draft-
ed, one could stay home. So I said to Emmitt right out, 'Emmitt,
you better be the one to go, you're always so restless anyway, driving around fast cars and all.' I told him a good joke that I thought
would make him have a sense of humor about it. I told him, 'Join
the Navy and See the World!'"

Mrs. Graving paused to let Mary laugh, but Mary was hung over
and had laughed at jokes all night at the V.F.W. Lounge, and a

childhood friend had tried to skin her in business, and she decided she didn't have to get up a laugh.

"Anyway," her mother-in-law went on, "he may not have had much sense of humor about going into the Navy, but he really enjoyed it once he got in. He must have, because he never wrote any homesick letters. He didn't ever write at all. Home never meant anything to him, like it did to Cordell. Cordell always had more plans, anyway. Dad and I helped him. We helped him buy all that lake frontage and that resort in Wisconsin that you were so set on having."

"I never heard of any Wisconsin resort," Mary said.

"I'm tired of people lying to me," Mrs. Graving said. "First that manager, Dahle, and now you. We paid all your doctor bills, too. All them bills, and there was never anything the matter with you that I could see."

"I never had any doctoring bills," Mary said. "I never went to a doctor, except for when the children came. You're probably thinking of Cordell's ulcer treatment."

"I gave my son," Mrs. Graving said conclusively.

Outside the glass doors of the Vision Avenue Apartments, Mrs. Blatke and Gregsy Hanson, who had once been a Faith Lutheran Church Release Time student of Mary's, were shouting at each other on the sidewalk. Mr Dahle, the building manager, stood by, wringing his hands. An interested circle of elderly residents had gathered. They murmured "Ohh!" and "Goodness!" from time to time.

"Oh, hi, Mrs. Graving," Gregsy said, breaking off.

"Oh, so it's 'Hi, Mrs. Graving,' is it?" Mrs. Blatke screeched. "But when I want to park my car in the parking place, he won't move his damned bike. Well, I'm asking you, 'Mrs. Graving,' since he seems to like you so much, who is that boy? I'm calling the police."

"Yeah, and I won't tell you," Mary heard herself saying.

"You going to take up for some kid who busted one of my headlights, are you? You going to take up for some kid against me?"

Mary said to herself, I might as well get into a fight as not. I really might as well.

"He's a friend of mine," she said aloud. Then she said, "You owe him an apology, too." She watched the woman's wrath with satisfaction.

"Apology? *Apology*? Me apologize to that crummy kid?"

"You threw his bike down on the sidewalk," Mary said. "I saw you."

"Well, did you see what he done to my car?"

It was bad. Gregsy Hanson or somebody had thrown a stone right into the left front headlight. For some reason—from pure force and accuracy, probably—the stone was still stuck in the shiny reflector of the light.

"You tell me the kid's name, or I'll call the police!" cried Mrs. Blatke. "They'll make you tell."

"They won't make me do anything," Mary said. Suddenly she felt very hung over. She said, "Maybe your other headlight will get busted by somebody."

"Ladies! Ladies!" cried Mr. Dahle, grasping one earlobe desperately. "Please—I've called the police—they'll be here—please, *please*! Here they come now!"

It was Merle Schaefer. Mrs. Blatke ran over to his police car and shouted that Mrs. Graving had just threatened to break one of her headlights and that kid there had already busted the other one.

"What kid is that, then?" Merle inquired, getting out of the car languidly.

The three of them turned and saw Gregsy Hanson now pedalling up Vision Avenue, away from them, and throwing rolled-up copies of the *Duluth Herald* at doorways as he went.

"And anyway, she's crazy!" Mrs. Blatke shouted, pointing at Mary. "I know she's crazy because she goes and visits them people at the Lutheran Social Service on Thursdays. Everybody's seen her."

Merle looked at Mary thoughtfully and then he turned to Mrs. Blatke. "Funny—I already told you, just today," he said. "You don't call a policeman, remember? You forget awful quick, Mrs. Blatke. Now, you listen to me. When you get home this afternoon and you see a big ape there, two storeys high, and this big ape climbs in your living-room window and swipes your TV and then it goes in your refrigerator and eats everything you got there, including the ice cubes, *you don't call a cop*! You understand that, now? You will get me in trouble yet."

Mr. Dahle now held up his hands in a position exactly like the framed "Praying Hands" picture that hung in his office. "I think we can all go back in now," he said in a high, gentle voice. "I think the show is over." He giggled.

Nobody who came to the Faith Lutheran Church to see a counsellor or therapist on Thursdays parked their car in the church parking lot. They parked across the street by the hospital, at the "Visitors" sign, and then walked over to the church. It didn't do any good. Everyone knew exactly who had nerves and who was crazy in Rachel River. It didn't matter about the wives of Duluth Airbase personnel; no one cared if they were crazy or not. But everyone knew exactly who the others were. Anyone who used the visiting psychotherapeutic services offered once a week by Lutheran Social Service was crazy or nervous. If they had a decent job, they had nerves; if they were on welfare, they were crazy. Mary Graving was just nerves, they guessed.

Now Mary sat, facing north, in the Sunday-school room where she had taught Release Time Religion, years before. The window faced the forest, where there were still wild animals living. One spring, twenty years ago or more, when men who had come back from one war or another still felt purposeful when they were gathered in groups, someone in town had spread it around that you would get a bounty if you went into those woods and brought out two fox's feet. All that summer, people killed foxes; there was near and distant firing almost every day, and traps set everywhere. Men referred to the animals—as people always do, for some reason, when they intend to kill a lot of them—in the collective. "There's a lot of fox in there," they remarked to each other on Main Street. "a lot of fox and some bear, but not so much bear as fox," instead of saying "A lot of foxes and some bears."

"I want to tell you something," Mary said to Jack, the therapist she saw every Thursday. "But before I tell you that, thinking of bears—out there—reminds me of something else I'll tell you."

She told the therapist about the young man baking bread in the Ye Olde 61. She described his strong elbows and his arms, how they smelled of whole-wheat flour, and how he braced them strongly on the table so they were next to her face, while they all looked out the window at a bear. She told how she had sat there talking business with the other man, and this man had come and leaned over their table, and how all of a sudden there was this tremendous, irresponsible, unaccountable, absolutely unforeseeable desire, all because of this man leaning over while they looked at the bear. She told Jack how they all looked at the bear, which wasn't really that interesting but they quit talking and watched it, and then suddenly this man with his arms covered with bread dough—a man whose name she didn't even know—said, "Do you see how when a bear moves it is more like dancing than when a dog moves?"

"Well," Mary said now, "well, when he said that—Well, the way he said it—Well . . ." She went on explaining, failing to explain it. "That part about the bear," she said at last, "that *dancing*—that finished me off!"

They both laughed, but then the therapist waited, deliberately making a pause too serious to be filled with conversations about bears.

"Well—and then I lied to you last week," Mary said. "And this is what I am celebrating. I told you I would not commit suicide because of the children. That is not the reason I won't commit suicide! I was wrong. I won't do it because of this thing I am celebrating. You see, I thought all life was of the creature, life of the body, and I felt I am dead in my body—yet I am not dead. So therefore I thought I would do a test. I would see if life is all life of the body or not. So I took nearly all the week and went back over, in my memory, all the body life I have ever had. I went back over how it was with every man I could remember—well, at least, every time I could remember!"

This explanation seemed grandiose, and Mary became anxious because she knew that patients waste half the time in sexual bragging, so she said, "I went over some of the times, anyway, and I made myself remember everything, just as if it were now. I went through the births of the children all over again. Exactly as if it were happening now. I remembered every detail of the labor and the delivery—and oh, after the delivery!—of both children, and of beginning to nurse them in the hospital, and singing to them. 'Annie Laurie' I sang—not the first verse, which is dumb, but the other two—remembering to sing very quietly because you can tell a baby's ears are not yet spoiled by bad sounds. You can tell by that nearly mashed, delicate-looking way the ears lie close to their heads. The way they lie mashed back against their heads like that, you can tell they have heard only the most wonderful sounds, like sounds from underwater. . . . So I went back over all that, and it was awfully sad. My God, it was sad. But it was not what I was grieving for. It wasn't!

"I felt sorry for myself and for everyone else in the meantime, because if it is physical delights we live for, we certainly don't get to spend our time in very nice places. We are always working in the basement, or drinking in the V.F.W., or washing things at the laundromat. The rich are the only ones that sail on beautiful lakes—and they call that 'touching down on reality.' Just yesterday, someone told me sailing was 'touching down on reality'—and all the while he was skinning me clean on a wholesale offer! Suddenly I realized I wasn't staying alive for my children. I was staying alive for something I haven't even begun to do yet. So I stopped being altruistic as if I were some saint, giving myself up for others. And I stopped thinking my life would be so different if only I could live in a cultivated place. Why do we praise children when they are willing to go into museums? So culture is nothing, I found out this week—nothing. It isn't why we live. And animal life—all that body stuff—that isn't it, either. It is something yet to do, something we're supposed to be doing in the future! But that's as far as I've got—I haven't looked at it any closer. I was simply so excited that I wasn't going to die, and that animal life is not all there is, that I went to the V.F.W. Lounge to get drunk and celebrate. And in there I listened to the men talking. They're in worse shape than I am, even—they thought World War Two was sort of a suit of armor, and now they don't know what they ought to be doing. Do you know that whenever I mention World War Two on my radio program five or ten of them, in this one little town alone, call me up and tell me things from their lives?

"And yet I had a terrible day, yesterday. Because I didn't know what life will be, and animal life has been taken away, and then even the new life, my life of thinking about suicide, was taken away. I was so empty then. I was horribly empty! So I got into a coarse street quarrel with a woman over a little boy. When he called me up later and said, 'Thank you for standing up for me,' it was as if somebody who was not anybody had stood up for him. I was simply emptied."

"But this week?" Jack said. "What about the suicide?"

"It's gone," Mary said. "But, do you know, I used to make special toys for the children—I still do. I am making a bookcase with a secret compartment. When I was sewing for them, or building something, I used to think, Well, then *this* is life. And I was wrong about that, too. Life for others isn't anything, either. Just as the rich are mistaken in thinking there is reality in sailing, the rest of us are mistaken in thinking there is reality in carpentry.

"So I think it is something we have to keep an eye out for—what we're supposed to do, why to stay alive. Do you sail, ever? Well, if you know small boats you know about keeping an eye out for the darker place on the water to windward, because the darker place, which keeps getting close, is what tells you how to trim differently. ... Well, that's enough!"

She stopped. Her facial tic reappeared now, and she controlled it.

"But it is wonderful, *wonderful*," she said, "to come here and tell you depressing stuff. Every day, I am cheerful on the radio, and people come up to me in Ben Franklin and say, 'Oh, you cheer us up so on the radio!' And my friends who are happily married come up and say, 'You do a terrific job of taking on that toy business so cheerfully!' We must be living in the most cheerful-minded century in the history of the world, even though the sheriff says the whole race is uniquely filthy!"

Mary and the therapist both laughed, and then they did serious work for the remainder of the session. She was not allowed then to divert from this serious work by telling stories about coarse women, or any of the other supposed facts of her life.

The Mouse Roulette Wheel

T HE ST. MATTHEW'S VESTRY had little in common; like most vestries, it was made up of rich men and poor men who were fortunately neither brave nor crazy, so they were able to carry on a nervous, lively conversation together. If the Senior Warden, a worn-out young man named Mosely, had been brave or crazy, he would have shouted at Forsyth: "It is infuriating! Infuriating that you work only three days a week, and sail your big shot boat the rest of the time! While I hold one full-time job and one part-time job and my wife has to help down at the Gopher Pantry — and we don't make a third of what you make! And that carpeting you sell — it's no good! You even sold the church bad carpeting!" Forsyth would have shrugged (if he, in turn, had been brave or crazy) and remarked, "Well, what do I care? You're just not somebody who'll ever make any money! You just aren't — well — you just aren't the kind of man that makes money — don't bleat!" But neither man said anything like that.

The six vestrymen were sitting in a little circle of folding chairs in the choir room, waiting to do the last planning of tomorrow's bazaar. It was Friday morning. They talked about fatal accidents together; they worked up to some gaiety about it, while their priest strode around the choir room behind them, finding the paper cups where someone had left them under a pile of surplices to be ironed. Father Bill gathered up easel and newsprint; he unplugged the coffeemaker and brought it over to the men.

They all liked Father Bill Hewlitt, who was forty-one. All their other rectors had been very young men who composed letters late at night to the Bishop, explaining that they surely enjoyed their rural parish work at St. Matthew's, Amos (Minnesota), but they were available for a metro parish if one should come free. What they liked especially about Father Bill was that he seemed content

to stay there in Amos. He belonged to them. So they felt he took
their church seriously.

Higgins was telling about a UCC minister from St. Anton Lake,
the next town, who had been called to the accident two weeks ago
on Minnesota 371 and Minnesota 200 and hadn't known the man
was dead. The conversation moved unerringly from mere death to
especially grisly death.

The little circle of men drew in; their voices sagged joyfully
lower. In 1975 Elmira Inman's half-brother fixed up a chainsaw to
the flywheel of his old John Deere and opened himself up all the
way lengthwise before they found him. Then there was that bal-
ing accident on the Pierce farm back before the law you had to use
string instead of wire. Before they found him, this man was half-
baled up as good as his own flaxstraw. And speaking of *finding*
people dead, Beske told how it was ten days before they found old
Wolfmeyer, not the one in the hospital now, but his cousin. He'd
been shooting in Amos Slough over near the Refuge and they
found him lying in the water. Those undertakers really knew their
job all right, Beske remarked. Amazing what they can do. Then
each man had a story about embalming or making up a face on top
of stocking plaster and how good they could make you look. Each
man waited sombrely for the man ahead of him to finish before he
would start his own anecdote.

Bill Hewlitt let it go until they got to the 1972 outboard motor
accident involving two young girls. Then he stalked over and said
firmly, "The Lord be with you." "And also with you," the men
had to return. They prayed and had to work fast to wind up all the
last-minute arrangements of the bazaar.

Bill served them as usual, standing at the newsprint, writing up
their comments, but he wasn't paying any attention. He was thinking of his older brother Francis, who was coming late that afternoon. They weren't close. They had scarcely seen each other since
they grew up—only once, six years ago, and the reunion had not
been successful. But now Francis had called from Washington, he
had chosen to come, he wanted to be met in Duluth in the old way,
and Bill found himself delighted.

He half-heard the vestrymen. They were now estimating to one
another which stall would make the most money at the bazaar. It
was always the mouse roulette wheel that made all the money. Men
gathered around it, watching the mouse moving, confused, with
that surprising liquidness of mice; and rolls of money passed
hands on the side, in addition to the pot St. Matthew's made on it.

Bill half-heard the vestrymen talking about it, but he was remembering dozens of the evenings of his adolescence in Duluth. He and his brother would steer their father's great Packard through the heavy fog off Lake Superior. They drove their father and his old friends home from their club. One by one the old men were let off at their houses, Francis sitting behind the wheel with the engine running, Bill jumping out and opening the car door. Sometimes a maid opened the lighted, oak door. She would stand to one side to let the old man go in, and then smile and greet Bill before he jumped back into the car. "Goodnight, Landers!" "Goodnight, Harris!" the old men still in the car would shout hoarsely, as they let off each man. Bill would jump back in, his face cleaned by the night fog; behind both boys, the men gradually sobered, coughing, belching quietly, bursting into little laughs over remarks remembered from the poker table.

In 1970, when their father was long dead, the house long ago sold, and all their father's gifts to them invested elsewhere, or in Bill's case, spent on seminary, Francis and Bill had one reunion. It was hastily got up. Francis had called Amos from Duluth and suggested Bill drive the two-hour trip in.

"Oh, but come out to us!" Bill had exclaimed. "You'll get to meet Molly! And come see the baby—and I'll show you my parish and all!"

"God, I'm sorry, Bill," Francis had said. "I just got in last night and I've been tied up all morning with conferences here—and I've got to get the morning flight back to Washington. Could you possibly get free and drive in? I'm at Landers's house—you remember Dad's old friend Landers? At least we can have a drink and go out for dinner somewhere."

Bill had obediently done the drive, at eighty miles an hour, arriving a half-hour before the time. Dazed by memories, he had driven up the curving asphalt driveway, between the perfectly groomed trees, each standing in its own circle of spaded earth. Then the house appeared, shockingly large, shockingly beautifully built of brick. "I'll tell them you're here, Father Hewlitt," the maid said.

He said, "Don't announce me. I'll just walk in. I'm early, but they expect me."

He went down a cool hallway. Men's voices rose from beyond double-doors ahead and to the right. "Oh, yes—I remember—the Landerses' livingroom was here—and to the right," Bill told himself.

The men's voices were triumphant, he thought, and excited. "I don't see any reason why that won't shape up at this end without any griefs," a strong voice said. That must be young Landers, Gorham or Gorston, whatever his name was. "I'll figure out a spread of regular American holdings for you, Fran," the voice went on. "We'll phase out the Anaconda or Kennecott or whatever touchy stuff you come in with—no matter how the politics go, and I'll check out my suggestions with you at that time. Now—on any extra cash input—"

"Sounds good, Gordy," another voice said, and Bill, pausing in the dark hallway felt his hair rise a little. My brother! he cried; he had thought he was looking forward to seeing Francis; now he *knew* he was looking forward to it more than he had begun to guess. In a single second, as a single impression, he thought: it is ridiculous for any men to be brothers for even five minutes—without being close! If it didn't come naturally, how did we fail to do it at least just as an act of will! What idiots! What a waste!

"Sounds good, Gordy," his older brother's voice was saying, adding with a laugh, "Christ! Chile could get to be a madhouse down there if it goes the way they think it will. And once more, Gordy, let me just say this might not amount to anything for you—or for me—but it could—it just could—go over the top of the page!"

A quiet rejoinder: "I'm indebted to you, Fran. Don't think I won't do my level best for you at this end."

Bill deliberately rattled the double-doors as he opened them. After the hallway so full of shadow, he was rather dazed by the white, opaque light in his face.

Beyond the room's immense window, Lake Superior lay covered with solid white fog. This fog filled the room with impersonal white light, neither cheering like sunlight nor doleful. Two men rose energetically from a long davenport in front of the window. Because they were in silhouette to Bill, he couldn't tell which one was his brother. Both came right towards him, stepping over the long coffee-table, both with right hands stretched to him.

"Bill Hewlitt, damn it! Marvelous!" cried Gordon Landers.

"Hello, Bill," said Francis. "It's been a million years."

They all stood shaking hands, touching one another's shoulders. "You remember baby Gordy Landers, that squirt kid we beat at Monopoly all the time?" Francis said, laughing.

"And look at Bill!" Gordy Landers said. "Clerical collar and all," said in a tone called respectful, which was in fact absolutely not respectful. Then, glancing down at the low table, which was neatly laid out with piles of papers, a china figure having been shoved down to one end, Gordon bent and began collating the papers into groups, and slipping them all into a chrome and leather case. He then poured a drink for Bill. Both men asked Bill if he wanted to be filled in on some one-liners from Washington. "It is my hope," Gordon said, handing Bill a highball glass, "That your brother doesn't darken our consulates and embassies in South and Central America with these stories. I'm encouraging him to get them all out of his system here!"

They all laughed and sat down.

This falling aircraft, Francis told them, had only three parachutes on board, but there were four passengers—three famous men and a Boy Scout. As President Nixon jumped out he grabbed a chute and shouted that he in particular should be a survivor for the sake of preserving the moral values of freedom and democracy in the Western World; then the second man, Kissinger, explained that he must survive as he represented the brains of the free world, and he jumped, leaving the Archbishop of Canterbury and the boy. The Boy Scout said reassuringly, "O go ahead, sir, take a chute. That last one grabbed my rucksack!"

Bill listened with a smile on his face, taking good strong sips of his scotch, thinking, how triumphant Francis's voice sounded! and, how cheerful these two guys sounded as he came in—how cheerful they still were!

But their cheer had to do with whatever their business was with each other. He felt good humor spilling over from both of them to him, but it was good humor left over from something that was nothing to do with him. They were both excited, they were in excellent humor with each other, and now they didn't want to be serious at all. They had obviously *been* serious; now the seriousness was used up and so their attitude was genial and playful.

Bill kept listening to his brother, thinking about him, gradually giving up any idea of a serious conversation. He kept on his face the amused, inquiring expression with which people listen to jokes, and he accepted some more drinks. After a while the scotch was comforting inside him and his face held its animated expression easily. The other men eventually asked him some questions about his life. Bill heard his own voice telling them about St. Matthew's Episcopal Church, about his wife Molly, about their year-old son and the baby expected midwinter. Then Bill longed to leave the huge sitting room lighted by the lake fog. He longed to drive home fast and angrily, yet somehow his voice kept talking

on, another ten, twelve minutes: he was even chattering. At one
point, unable to stop himself, he had even pulled out a picture of
Molly and little George. Part of him said, "Get up and go, you
great ass!" But another part of him kept him stuck, chattering
away at his well-travelled brother and that Landers kid who had
grown up into some kind of shrewd broker and exporter.

Hours later, driving gingerly through the cold night mist, Bill
had cried aloud in his car, remembering his garrulity.

Now, six years later, he was sure this visit would be entirely
different.

After the Vestry meeting, Bill had two appointments. Since the
first was not until two o'clock, he went across the St. Matthew's
lawn, had a look out over the sky-colored, slightly misty lake, and
entered his study, a small building attached to the rectory garage.
He pulled over the pile of letters to be answered.

The telephone rang. In the receiver, Bill heard gigantic background noise of steam and metal, then a very loud voice shouted
directly into his ear: "This is Elmira, Father Bill. We're getting a
lot of feedback down here in the kitchen. Some of them are saying
we ought to make the hamburgers bigger, the way they used to of,
but I said we ought to keep them in line with what they're serving
in uptown Amos. There's no point in making a lot of enemies for
nothing, Father. People don't need no big hamburgers if what
they're used to is what they're serving in the Gopher Kitchen and
they *been* serving and with this here inflating if we're going to
make a cotton-picking nickel off this bazaar—"

"Elmira," Bill said, imagining walking leisurely through the
bazaar tomorrow with his brother, imagining Francis with the
cordiality he had even as a teenager, squandering a mint at all the
food stands: "Elmira, let's go ahead and make the hamburgers
huge—wouldn't that be all right? Elmira, let's let the word get out
that the St. Matthew's Episcopal Church bazaar has the most
generous, most terrific hamburgers of any church in a twenty-mile
radius!"

"What about the money?" she said. Then there was a pause
during which Bill heard something like steam escaping from a
sinking liner. It was followed by a sharp hoarse cry from Elmira,
who had turned away from the receiver: "Louise, for cat's sake
don't grab that thing in yer bare hands," and then more sizzling as
if now an entire boiler had poured out onto hot metal. Someone,
no doubt Louise, Bill smiled to himself, trying to think, Louise
who? uttered from somewhere near the receiver a very clear rude
remark.

Bill said, "We aren't just giving away hamburgers! Great big good ones, Elmira! 50¢ each, not 10¢—we'll make money!"

"Okay, Father, you're responsible. It's over my dead body!"

He said with a laugh, "Oh, go on, Elmira, make them whatever size you think best."

Now his desk buzzer went off. The parish secretary, Coralie, said, "I've got Lorraine Mosely on the outside line, Bill."

"Oh, all right," Bill said gaily, thinking: only two more hours until I can get some tea with Molly and then go to the airport and pick up Francis.

"Father Bill," came Mrs. Mosely's sombre voice. She said very significantly, "I would like to *share* about Jesus at the bazaar tomorrow."

"No sharing at the bazaar," Bill said.

"I can't believe what I'm hearing, Father! I can't believe you're really saying to me that we wouldn't have sharing at a big gathering of Christians like that! In my Prayer Group they're already talking about our church! You know what they'll say, Father? They'll say, 'Yeah? Where else but at an Episcopal Church would you get together four or five hundred Christians without one mention of Jesus Christ during the whole thing?' is what they'll say."

Bill said, "We always have a blessing at every bazaar. So there will be mention of Jesus Christ. No sharing, Lorraine."

He was annoyed when his two o'clock appointment was still not there at ten after two. The young man who had called saying he wished to make a *confession* had said he would come by boat; so now Bill went outside, and waited, scowling, at the top of the rise over Lake Amos.

Bill knew him by name. He was Duane Wolfmeyer, the grandson of Neil Wolfmeyer, a very old parishioner now dying in Amos Hospital. The Wolfmeyers were a type of Episcopalian that exasperated most rectors; they showed up in church only for some baptisms, most marriages, and for their own funerals—for hitching and ditching, as people described it at Diocesan coffee breaks. But Bill felt comfortable with such people. His own parents had seldom gone to church. They were intellectuals, and if they sang every Christmas Eve mass, they were also given to describing Jesus as a megalomaniac on Low Sundays. Bill had not embarrassed his brother by inviting him to his ordination.

Now the young Wolfmeyer grandson followed Bill into his study, and wandered without shyness over to the bookcases. "What a terrific place you've got!" he said. "Terrific funky study, sir! I love it! Beautiful!! Beautiful!" The young man went easily around the room in his tennis shoes, touching bindings with tanned knuckles. "Christ, you've got everybody! Merton! Evelyn Underhill! Underhill's fantastic! Christ, you've even got volume eighteen of the collected Jung and I didn't even know it was out yet! And the *Bogi Hokjhar Shetar*! Terrific, Father Hewlitt!"

Bill had sat down at his desk. "Sit down, Duane," he said, after a moment. "Sorry," he added, aware that he didn't like the man at all and would have to consider that fact all the while they were talking. "This is one of those days when we have to run on schedule." Practically all the while he spoke, he kept looking out the window, nervous with pleasure, anticipating the drive into the city. The wonderful basswood forest, with its straight, black trunks and the clumsy leaves, so surprisingly clumsy and moving, was already going yellow although it was only the middle of August. The mist that had lain over the lake all morning now began to fill the woods. Its gentle windings were full of ease.

Duane Wolfmeyer had begun a long narrative of his life as a surveillance man for the C.I.A. He explained he had joined students' groups in Colorado, and also helped organize 4 x 6 cards on selected people around Boulder in particular. He had found the money useful, he explained, because he was doing some writing, and really more important, he said slowly, regarding the priest significantly, he was doing "a great deal of spiritual work." It was just so damned practical, he said to Bill, and frankly, he hadn't seen where anybody had been harmed by it. "What makes me mad at myself, though," Duane continued in a frank tone, smiling, "is that no one tried to deceive me about it. I knew perfectly well this guy came from an intelligence group and I knew what he wanted me to do—well, for starters anyway—to inform on those students' groups, and then he said they would see what else turned up. Sometimes weeks and weeks went by and there wasn't anything to do, but I still got paid. Obviously I knew I wasn't getting all that money for nothing. . . . still, I did it because it was so darn practical. It meant I didn't have to write home to my dad for money—and in a way, of course, it was really sort of a good thing. It gave me time to take in some Meditation, and I did a lot of really good reading, too. Father, would you mind if I smoked?"

"Yes, I'd mind," Bill said, looking out the window.

People kept going by, now, with paper flowers and twisted crêpe about their heads and necks. Some of them carried 2 x 4's for bazaar stalls, and large boxes which Bill knew were filled with fairly wretched Anglican trinkets. There were tiny nylon flags printed

with the Cross of St. George, which ravelled at a child's first handling of them; buttons to wear; magic tricks with a mother and
father rabbit made of felt. Duane Wolfmeyer's voice rose and fell.
He explained his experience as an informer over again, and then
over again, warming to it, using different reminiscences to illustrate.

The whole question of C.I.A informers was not new to Bill. The
year before he had discussed it around the dining room table at
Lane House, the Minnesota Diocesan headquarters, with five or
six priests. Bill had thought through the problem of C.I.A. people,
and faced with this problem he would tell the informer to work off
the bad job done, something like atonement.

There is no profession, Bill recalled leisurely from Conrad, deciding he would repeat it to Duane, that fails a man more completely than that of a secret agent of police. But when the priest
looked over at the courteous, relaxed, conversant young man in
front of him he realized: far from being *failed*, this fellow was not
even repentant. In fact, as he wound up, Duane was now suggesting that he was money ahead and to all intents and purposes, no
harm done.

"How many people have you told this to?" Bill now asked.

"Let's see," Duane said. "It's been a while now, you know. Let's
see. I did tell my apartment-mate at the time; but he said it was a
damned sight better than sweating a teaching assistantship. Then,
I told this Quaker workcamp leader that I'd worked with—that's a
man you'd like, Father Hewlitt. Then I did tell Rinpoché —that's
my meditation teacher. And I told a guy I knew that's a
Congregational minister."

"Anyone else?" Bill said.

"I'm trying to think," Duane said in a frank, cooperative voice.
"O yes! I participated in a Massich Group seminar and during
Sharing I think I may have mentioned something . . ." He added,
"People have been helpful."

"But you still want my opinion?" Bill said, smiling slightly.

"Yes, sir—it's why I came, I guess."

Bill looked out the window. "The important thing is that the
conversations now come to an end. You've had enough talk. What
I think, what your roommate thinks, what the Friends Service
Committee man thinks, and so on—all that is past now. Now you
need to *do* something."

"I would like to hear any suggestions you have," Duane said.
"My grandfather thinks very highly of you, sir."

"First," Bill said, now turning from the window, "I suggest you simply obey all the advice you've ever received on the subject. If the Buddhist gave you some exercise or discipline to do, do it. Do whatever the Quaker told you to do. Whatever the Congregational minister told you to do, do that. Then I want you to do what I'm about to tell you to do, too. The point is, Duane, to do something, do something. The talking is over—forever. You absolutely must not tell any more people about it. Not one. If you meet a girl, don't tell her."

"Wow," said Duane. "For sure?"

"For absolute sure," Bill replied. "You've talked enough. From now on you carry it alone. Now—do you want to hear the rest?" He smiled. "Or is that enough?"

"No, hell, please," Duane said. "Please go on."

"You were well paid," Bill said. "Add up as well as you can the actual number of hours you worked as an informer and write it down. Then work it off, hour for hour, at volunteer work, scratching off each hour in some simple, completely visible way—such as on paper or wood. This will show you that *that* mark on the left, say, was an hour of bad work, this mark through it, on the right, is an hour of *good* work. This will give you some secret structure of your own. It'll also help you," Bill added wryly, "not to take another job of the same kind—which they would probably offer you on a higher level this time."

"You don't mind laying it on a person, Father Hewlitt!"

"Well," the priest said mildly, "did you tell them you would never work for them again?"

"Well, no," Duane said.

"That's all I meant," Bill said glossily.

After another moment he threw Duane Wolfmeyer out because he was expecting a ten-year-old acolyte named LeRoy Beske who had called for an appointment.

When LeRoy showed up at the screen door, Bill got up and opened it for him, and shook his hand. He pointed out to him a gigantic chair placed for guests. "I'm glad the mist is coming up again, LeRoy," Father Bill said. "I've always liked fog. I was brought up in it. In fact, in the harbour of my city, Duluth, there used to be this big foghorn that bellowed like a sick cow all night and half the morning all summer—to keep oreboats from smashing into the bridge, I suppose. Come on in."

"But that fog better not ruin the bazaar tomorrow, though." LeRoy said. "My mother baked all them pies; she's going to go straight up if that bazaar gets called off."

"And your dad's got the David-and-Goliath slingshot booth this year?" Bill said.

"Yeah," LeRoy said.

LeRoy didn't seem to be getting around to what he wanted to say so Bill offered, "Well, last year's slingshot booth was crooked. You couldn't knock the targets down with a roadpaver."

"It's cleaned up this year, sir," LeRoy said. "And I wanted to tell you something, sir. We want to clean up the mouse roulette wheel game."

"Fill me in on the whole thing," the priest said.

"It's the mice for the men's mouse wheel," LeRoy said. "They have this wood roulette wheel, you know the one, Father; they made it about a yard across and painted into all these pie-wedge piece shapes, red, orange, like that. Then all around the outside edge it's got these holes cut out, same size as a beer can. They have the cans stuck onto the wheel, under the holes, so when they spin the wheel, they drop the mouse on it, and when he gets sick or something, he dodges into one of them holes and then whatever man got bets on that color of a hole, he gets half the pot and St. Matthew's gets the other half, is how it works. Anyhow, the problem is this is a very popular thing at the bazaar, Father, like you get ten, twelve men standing around paying into the roulette wheel all the time and we sometimes have to kind of force people to hang around the slingshot booth and the other games. You know, Father, I seen you herding bunches of ladies over to the booths a lot of times."

Bill winced.

"Here, Father, we got this here for you." LeRoy stood up and wrestled a piece of paper out of his jeans pocket.

PROTEST AGAINST MOUSE ROLET WHEEL

Bill read at top, and under it:

> We the undersined protest the mouse rolet wheel because it is mean to the mice. Also it isn't just one mouse, they use a lot of them. We think it should be stopped. Sined:
>
> Janet Higgins, E.S.N. Forsyth, Brett Forsyth, Verona Mosely, and LeRoy Beske.

With the lightning speed of an experienced rector, Bill noted that all the names belonged to children of his strongest churchmen—vestry members, Sunday School teachers, tithing donors, the Senior Warden. Terrific, he said to himself with a sigh.

When he was alone again, Bill looked at his appointments list and wrote "See about mice" opposite LeRoy's name. He could still hear Duane Wolfmeyer's boat engine and picked up the phone.

When the nurse on duty at the hospital answered, he said, "This is Father Hewlitt, Debby. How is Mr. Wolfmeyer doing?"

"Holding his own, Father. We'll keep you in touch."

This whole pleasant world of forest and lake where Bill was rector of St. Matthew's Episcopal Church was tottering now, nearly wrecked. Whenever Bill looked out over the peaceful water he was aware, for example, that Lake Amos, which looked so immutable, showed in fact on engineers' maps in St. Paul as part of the gated chain of lakes which could be tapped, opened, whenever Minneapolis and St. Paul needed water. Bill was aware, too, that four sharp young Episcopalians who had summer places on Lake Amos, and who showed up every Sunday for church and could always be counted on for the alto, tenor, and bass of Vulpius, Williams, and Bach were all of them counsel for mining interests in Duluth and Scranton. These companies laid out schedules for years and years ahead, showing when they would begin to take the ore under Lake Amos. Their public relations departments projected a timeline for publicity to inure the public to the stripping when it came. The photograph was to suggest bliss; it would show young and middle-aged people, sailing well hiked out on Lasers, men and women in golden lifebelts, plenty of sky, plenty of very clear water—the overall tone much like that of the flowery-meadow photographs utilities firms used when they were telling Americans how the west would look again—after all the coal had been taken.

Bill knew that family corporation offices in Duluth kept huge stiff maps with pale blue lines on them, like the veinwork of tiny animals. The legends of these maps were written beautifully, in a surprisingly feminine hand, like the legends on treasure maps in children's books. These huge maps were opened out onto standing-height lecterns to fee owners like old Neil Wolfmeyer, Bill's parishioner, who now lay dying in the hospital. Elderly women laid their sky-color gloves to one side of the map and asked their executors to show them the reserve mine known as Wiggin-Amos No. 5. These people had very likely not heard of the town of Amos, Minnesota, itself, and certainly not of St. Matthew's Episcopal Church, with its cheap, carpeted rectory and its rector's study tacked to the garage and the bright grass running down the lake, and its altar still smelling of incense on Monday mornings. Yet all this lay over their holdings.

Each morning in August, the lake gave comfort like granite, under its mist. One felt the easy presence of old, uneducated men fishing, scarcely moving their wrists over the worn boats' edges. There was ease in how the line lay over their bent index finger, pinned by the thumbnail, and ease in how the line dropped with no movement into the water.

Bill's parish was half such people—a local populace that could still make a living in the wooded country. They serviced snowmobiles, ordering parts from Brainerd; they ran roadside plumbing repair services; they tongue-and-grooved logs for cabins. The other half were the rich, who bought up the failed dairy farms.

Finally Bill got into the car for the two hours' drive to Duluth Airport. He travelled in a lovely mist. It was impossible to feel that this wild country of Minnesota was endangered. Among the basswood trees must be dusk enough and room enough for millions of mice and impractical ferns to find some sort of a living. What is interesting, Bill thought, is how we all secretly want these to outlive our species, mankind, because they are nicer. He drove in an alien, fresh way, enjoying car and mist.

At the airport he stood around for a while near four or five other people.

"Nah, you can tell he's a Catholic," a woman's voice said expertly, somewhere behind Bill.

"Nah, he isn't though," another woman's voice said, with exactly the same intonation of expertise. "He's an Episcopalian, I know, because he's from my home town."

Now a crowd was growing around Bill; the air filled with the incoming jet's shriek. Everybody seemed pleased with the noise. People lifted up on the balls of their feet, and leaned over other people's shoulders. The air carried a waft of fuel oil, and close at hand, chewing gum.

The passengers began coming into the waiting room. The very first man made Bill lurch forward a little, it seemed so like a thinner, older type of Francis; then Bill saw it wasn't he and began studying the others as they came off. That's right, he considered, Fran would take his time. He would not muscle into the aisle. It would be like him to help ten women get their coats down from among the pillows overhead. So Bill was waiting composedly when a hand touched his shoulder. He turned to see a shocking, emaciated face. It belonged the first man he had seen come up the ramp, his brother Francis.

They shook hands in the old way, then drew back, their hands now fallen to their sides. They had never embraced and they didn't now. Bill saw instantly that Francis was dying, and the brother saw that Bill saw it and nodded. "Give me the baggage tags," Bill said, in a shepherding gesture he would not have made otherwise.

They stood waiting for the baggage, as rigidly and normally as they could. Their eyes were silver-coated with tears. Everything they saw was zigzag and crystal with tears, but Bill darted forward at the right moment, grabbed the bags, took Francis to the car, and they drove away.

II

When men and women think of becoming Episcopal priests they tend to imagine themselves in heavy, quiet rectories, with small panes at the windows—but in real life, a Minnesota rector is often proudly offered a modern, gimcrack ranchhouse. The sashes swell quickly after every rain.

Bill and Molly's rectory was carpeted with speckled aqua nylon from room to room. The speckled aqua was endless. It led out to the guest room on the first floor; it led up the staircase to the second; it led to the kitchen, where it joined a speckled aqua linoleum meant to suggest piazza tiling. At all the windows hung drapery in a complicated pattern called "Florentine," which the St. Agnes' Guild had voted for 12 to 3. A giant wooden salad fork and spoon were pinned at a certain angle to the wall. Things broke rather easily. Then the vestry came and peered, especially Hayden Forsyth, whose firm had laid the carpet. Sometimes three or four women arrived in a flurry to "see about those drapes." They gently lifted and set things down. "I remember the year we all made these!" someone would exclaim, holding up a rose-colored artfoam doily, scalloped at the edges, on which one was to set a figurine or a bowl of plastic fruit. All about the room were gifts to priest and family from one parishioner or another.

Molly and Bill made a joke of all this for Francis. It was Saturday morning, the day of the bazaar. They were sitting in the living room rather surprisingly early. Molly had expected the sick man to be tired from travel, and to sleep late, while she and Bill caught a moment of peace before the day was on them. But, in fact, like many people in crisis, Francis was highly charged. He had waked many times in the night and finally allowed himself to rise at six-thirty, wishing not to disturb anyone. When he came into the living room, all dressed, and found Bill and Molly already there, with a coffee urn between them, an expression of euphoria lighted his face. They both saw instantly that he had had a bad night and was delighted it was over. Bill held him out a thin, flowered cup, from a set the little boys were not allowed to handle, and thought: this is my blood relative—how nice he is here. Everyone smiled at every single remark made. Molly understood it was a crisis—everyone understood.

The telephone and the doorbell rang at the same moment. Molly went to the door, Bill to the phone. Molly returned with a beaming, respectful young man. "This is Duane Wolfmeyer, Francis. My husband's brother, Duane—Francis Hewlitt. He just flew in from Washington last night."

"Good to meet you, sir," Duane said, reaching across the coffee table to shake hands. Francis half-rose and then sank down again.

"Are you one of my brother's parishioners?" Francis said, smiling.

"Not exactly. I came over early to see if I could help with any last minute things about the bazaar. I'm just visiting my grandparents' home here, and Father Hewlitt has been wonderful to my grandfather, who's sick."

Francis said, "I never darkened the door of a church when I was a young fellow. I don't think I'd have known what a bazaar was, much less offer to help at one." He crossed his legs. "Can't say I missed it."

The younger man caught the tone of superior, more manly activity than his own. He didn't sit down at all.

Bill appeared quickly from the kitchen doorway. He had a white stole slung over one shoulder and he carried his communion box in one hand. With the other he fumbled at the stole, putting the lavender side neatly under, the white up. "How are you today, Duane?"

The gathered, competitive expression Duane had worn with Francis Hewlitt disappeared; now he looked vulnerable, in the way of people who have been counselled. "Can I drive you?" he begged.

"Nope, but thanks," Bill said, leaving. "Why don't you stay? You can get filled in on United States South American policy from my brother here."

Molly followed Bill to the car.

"I'm taking communion to old Wolfmeyer," he said, putting the box into the front seat, and sliding in after it. They talked for a moment, the idling car sounding very modern, very mechanical, the man in the lace-edged stole looking very old-fashioned.

When Bill returned an hour later everyone was at work on the bazaar. Francis had helped the people raise a makeshift flagpole at the beach, with the Episcopal flag—cross of St. George in red, the white background, the baby-blue field with nine small crosses—and now it was fluttering over the dock. Francis held cordon for little girls who were threading it through the wobbly stancheons to make the David-and-Goliath slingshot shy. A Lutheran electrician had kindly offered to arrange the outdoor wiring. Bill noticed that the summer people, who were lawyers, stockbrokers, and retired people, and all-year-round people were working together with jerky gaiety. They seemed to like handling the rougher, poorer poles, blocks, bolts; when something broke from old age, such as tent ropes, they noisily got up ingenious ways of making do. This aspect of the bazaar always made Bill grumpy. He found their cameraderie phony. After every bazaar the people said, "How wonderful the way it brought us all into closer fellowship!" But Bill knew that the three men and one woman lawyer, who were asking LeRoy Beske (as they all worked setting up a water tank for the Senior Warden to be dumped into) how you could tell a Polish bachelor's bathtub from a French bachelor's bathtub, would return on Monday to plan tax benefits for mining interests. These mining operators would strip off not just LeRoy Beske's dad's trailerhouse lot, with its bit of jackpine scrub; they would also strip off the cemetery where LeRoy Beske's grandparents' bodies lay shrinking.

At lunchtime the Hewlitts had only tea, because they must eat bazaar food literally all afternoon. Francis was in the guest room with his door closed. The little boys looked at Bill, from where they sat on either side of Molly, afraid he would interrupt the story she was reading aloud.

"Keep reading," Bill said, smiling. He lay back in his chair and listened to how Trouble dogged one brother until that brother at last tricked Trouble into a hole with a heavy stone near by, then rolled the stone over so Trouble couldn't get out. But the other brother nagged the first brother to tell him where the treasure lay; finally, the younger explained that one must roll aside such and such a stone. The older brother raced over and heaved away the stone; Trouble leapt out and rode on *his* back for the rest of his days. Since that was the venal, wicked, elder, cruel, mean, coarse, uncaring and unscrupulous brother, the little boys were immensely pleased, and they bent over Howard Pyle's illustrations carefully. They loved all the tricking and lying, they loved the plain greed, and then they loved justice winning in the end.

Outside, the loudspeaker which was to play waltzes all afternoon had been hooked to its tree. Someone asked it over and over, "Testing?" Inside, the house was introverted and calm; even the bad furniture looked heavy, and calm, and decent.

Bill and Molly talked lazily, putting off gathering their cheer and general affection to go outside. The children had toppled over on Molly's knees, beautifully asleep like baby birds. The door-bell rang. Duane Wolfmeyer came into the room. Everyone whispered so the little boys could sleep another few moments. At last Bill stalked out to find a clean collar, and returned, still fastening it.

"If there's anything I can do at all?" the younger man said, following the priest with his eyes.

"Duane told Francis that the C.I.A. was a very bad organization," Molly said, smiling. "You should have heard him!"

"I thought I told you to keep quiet about the C.I.A.," Bill said. "In fact, that was the first thing I told you to do, was *shut up* about the C.I.A."

"Sorry, Father Hewlitt, but frankly, your brother kind of *drew* me. He kind of surprised it out of me. He was so interesting, talking about places he's been and things he's done—and the people he knows, my God. And then I was so surprised when he said he's been associated with C.I.A. projects from time to time—I'm afraid he surprised it out of me, sir."

Molly and Bill both looked up. "Oh, I doubt he had much to do with an organization like that," Molly said at last, in the tone she used to break up quarrels in the St. Agnes' Guild. "I don't think I heard him say anything like that—of course I wasn't there all the time you two were talking."

Duane said agreeably, "Oh, he didn't do a lot. Mostly he just arranged premises for them in different places at different times. It sounds a lot more interesting than most jobs I've heard of. He said he just did useful things, like, if they needed a small import firm in Santiago, say, for engineering equipment, he'd see that one got set up. That sort of thing."

Feeling confident, and seeing that he had their interest, Duane remarked, in a manly way putting down any emotional aspects, "No, I doubt he did any very exciting cloak and dagger stuff. He

said himself—as if it were just a joke—that he was hardly much of
an asset to them. Mostly he told them the places he's been with the
State Department—Athens, Cambodia, Mexico City, Santiago. I
hope I wasn't rude, Father Hewlitt, but I did share your thought
about moral responsibility. Sorry, sir."

Now the hall door opened. "Well!" Francis Hewlitt cried, raising his hand in pretend Buckingham Palace salute. "I'm ready to
do the bazaar, by God! I've promised George and Timmy I'll buy
them three shots at every single game in the place, and two hamburgers apiece, if you're selling 'em anywhere!"

He had rested. He must have rinsed his ill face with hot and cold
water: he looked shining and friendly, and he had combed his always handsome hair into a neat wave. Francis wore a white linen
coat and an ivory polo shirt. He gave off a kind of blazing good
will that nearly hid the dreadful look of illness.

They woke the children. Everyone went outside. A little numbly,
they began to go about the bazaar. The Strauss played from the
loudspeakers. Women already sitting at TV tables overlooking
Lake Amos caught Bill by the elbow and one cried, "Oh, Reverend
Hewlitt? Oh, Reverend! This is something you Episcopalians do
so well!" Near the garage someone in a Midwest, nasal accent
began to do a good job of squawking Punch's voice as he threatened
the baby. The Senior Warden, a rich carpet salesman from Minne-
tonka, perched fully dressed on the edge of a drum full of water. He
was ready to be promptly dropped in if you threw a ball so it tripped
the mechanism.

Down on the beach there were a few people taking the sailboat
rides, but mostly, their owners conversed quietly at buoy. They were
middle-aged men and women whose fingers kept touching along
the stays and shrouds even when they were just waiting for riders.
Most of the young people leaned, smiling and commenting, over
Duane Wolfmeyer's big Crestliner.

Duane now wore a button that read KISS ME I WENT TO THE
ST. MATTHEW'S BAZAAR. He ambled down to the dock and
took all the kids out in groups of four. All the rest of the afternoon
the big boat's roar went around the lake. The waltzes kept tinkling
out of the birch leaves.

Bill was drawn into groups here and there; he could be seen
everywhere, rocking on his heels, his head bent to listen, his face
getting sunburnt afresh over the black shirtfront. "You don't
know me, Father Hewlitt," a woman cried, placing boneless fingers
on his arm. "But I have always admired you and your nice wife and

when I saw you at the airport yesterday in Duluth I said to my cousin who was with me, 'Why, that's our Episcopal priest from Amos, of all people; I'd know him anywhere!' I was meeting my sister." Bill shook hands with everybody; he laughed at all the jokes.

III

Sooner or later they were going to have to have a serious conversation. The dread of it began at supper and clung to them all, except the children. When Molly had read to the boys and put them to bed, she returned to the living room where they all sat a moment, watching the evening mist rising from the lake. For them all, they felt, it was the blessed evening after enforced cheer. Whatever communal dancing meant to Breughel, church carnivals don't mean that now.

Francis set his own stage. He had offered to lay the fire himself, and now he lighted it, and then moved deftly around the room. He brought in from his suitcase expensive liqueur which Bill and Molly would never keep. He had gone and poked about in the kitchen until he found some glasses stuck behind a pile of 9 x 13 cake pans with women's names printed on adhesive-tape on them. He brought out a brass tray painted with orange wavy lines, on which stood six thinnish glasses, also painted with orange wavy lines—a gift from someone in the parish.

"Well," Francis said, looking briefly into both their faces, and then addressing the fire in a light, ordinary tone: "Actually this isn't just regular United States leave for me. In fact—in fact, as I think you have guessed, I retired. About two weeks ago. I've been more or less taking care of details. The Bethesda apartment. That sort of thing." There was a pause. Then Francis said, "I have a serious health problem." Another pause. "The fact is, I've got a prognosis of either six weeks or longer that'll be what the doctor calls 'good' weeks, and it might last longer but she didn't think so. So here is my plan, and I want your opinion of it. See what you think! And if you know a better alternative, for God's sake, tell me." He kept talking, in a practical, expressionless tone, making it unnecessary for them to interject pity. "I thought I'd spend the six weeks here—oh, not at your house!" he said with a grin. "In a rented cabin—all arranged with some people I met at your bazaar this afternoon! Rather neatly, if I say so myself!"

"But Francis," Molly said. "we'll take care of you."

"That's another thing," he replied. "I don't know how much trouble I'll be—maybe not much—certainly there shouldn't be any problem for a bit; and then, when there is, I'll head for the hospital."

"We'll fill all the gaps, Fran," Bill said. "And Fran, you haven't said what you've got, but I take it it's been properly looked at? And if there's a course of treatment you're doing it . . . ?"

"I've been the route," Francis said wryly.

"Well then," Molly said, "I can see why for the while you'd rather be alone in peace and quiet. But if you get sick and don't want to be all the way across in Amos or wherever you've gotten the cabin, come to us. It won't always be quiet, but sometimes it will be quiet—and we're here."

Francis smiled at her, then turned to Bill and said, "I rather like the idea of my own family seeing me through like this. We haven't done that much, have we?" He looked pointedly at Bill's collar, and the cross hanging on his chest. "You might even do your thing with me."

No matter how decidedly Francis had told them his news, no matter that they had been accustomed to the idea of his sickness for a day and a night, they were still all stiff and motionless, like people making a point of sitting bolt upright, although in fact they were lounging backward in sofa and chairs. The sense of Francis's death floated into everyone.

"Well," Francis said, "that isn't all I came to tell you about. That was the bad news, as the kids say! Here's the good news! You think of me," he said in a witty tone, "as just a stodgy member of the United States State Department, bent over my desk during the siesta hours, filling in the mindless evenings under the Southern Cross in white tie, telling Polish jokes to the wives of dictators so they will understand our democratic culture—"

Molly and Bill smiled dutifully.

"But actually," Francis went on, "I have built up a little port-folio of sorts—nothing momentous, mind you—but it's all look-ing in fair shape now anyway, and since I don't seem to have a spouse to leave it to—I would like to leave it to you and your little tigers George and Timothy." He kept talking so they would not have to express any gratitude immediately. "It's a mix," he was say-ing. "Some mining stuff—some of the obvious things—we can go into all that tomorrow. And in Duluth, on Monday, I have an ap-pointment with a guy named Gordon Landers: Bill, do you remember Gordy Landers? He will fix it all up for you, in trusts or whatever you think best—some of it was guesses I don't mind saying have worked out pretty well! Nothing to challenge the Arabs with, but enough for four years apiece at Harvard or wherever for both kids, unless the country goes absolutely crazy—crazier than we are already," he added genially, loping on casually in his monologue in the able way of people accustomed to taking meetings through their agenda.

But even Francis, who had spent half a lifetime conversing with uncongenial people in crisis situations, could not be expected to gabble on and on. "Well, hell," he said, eventually, "you guys could say *some*thing, anyway." Then he added neatly, "Oh, and the portfolio was worth one and one-half million this morning."

Francis leaned back looking ill and also pleased with himself, his pale hands upright, prayer-fashion, on the manila envelope. Bill knew he was thinking: it isn't every day an Anglican priest with a two-bit parish in the middle of the Minnesota northwoods gets a cool million and a half in stocks dumped into his skinny lap. Bill waited until he controlled the stiffness in his throat and then said, "Listen, Francis, you told Duane Wolfmeyer something about the C.I.A. this morning ... I gathered you had done some work with them? I'd like to hear about that."

"Oh, for the love of Christ," Francis said in a bored way.

"Molly and I were very surprised," Bill said. "We didn't know you were doing anything like that."

"Ah, that drip Duane," Francis said. "You have a marvelous patience about you, Bill. You must have dozens of people like that Duane hanging around. But you keep up a straight face with him! And you, too, Molly! I'm all respect! I have to confess we talked for about twenty minutes and then I more or less told him to go to hell—or at least not to wax so damned moral before breakfast. I'll tell you one thing we really do learn as we get older: we learn not to be in such brilliant form before breakfast! It's an imposition on the other human beings in the room!"

"He said you told him you had done work for the C.I.A.," Molly said.

Francis gave her the smile that confident men save for unpleasant women. "And so I have," he replied mildly. "Most infrequently, I may add, and admittedly, nothing very interesting. I was hardly what they call an asset. It's just that my face logically belonged in certain places at certain times, so I could manage trivial arrangements without fuss. I'm no expert, you know. I suppose they make

use of a few thousand people like me from time to time. I am sure
the Soviet Union does the same sort of thing," Francis added
sensibly.

"One and a half million dollars," Molly said. "You must be on
the receiving end of something very big!"

"Let me relieve your mind, Molly," Francis interrupted, keeping a firm, still affectionate tone. "There is no way—please know
this!—there's no way the most corrupt broker with the most inside
information in the world could parlay a $10,000 inheritance—the
same as your Bill here got—into one and a half million on the
fluctuations of Kennecott, ITT, or Anaconda or anyone else's
stock—at least not while I was in the area."

"Then how'd you make it?" Bill said.

Francis said coolly, "I arranged for importation of heavy machinery into Chile. They needed it. Does that sound terribly
wicked?"

Francis now tapped the manila envelope on his knees. "I think
there are a couple of things," he said, "that you two had better
think about before you ask such holy questions about where I got
what, whom I've been consorting with—all questions that are very
easy to ask. There are other questions, it seems to me, that you
haven't asked, such as: what makes you think Timmy and George
will want to go to Bemidji State or Brainerd Vo-Tech and marry
someone who will nail up plastic salad spoons and forks on the
walls, and khaki reproductions of the Praying Hands? You two
make a joke of it, but you *chose* this life! And, you chose this life
after you tucked away Harvard and lots else of the world! I'll hand
it to you," he said, a smile returning to his face, "there's some sort
of moral force in your life—but you might well find that Tim and
George will have their own ideas. And I don't want to imply that
you just live a simple, easy existence out here, Bill, with nothing
worse to fret about than a morning's quarrel with your vestry, but
frankly—and Molly, you ought to think about this, too—there are
a lot of tough people around in some unpleasant places, some in
danger all the time, and these very tough people are looking out
for *your* well-being. If some of these people—and now we are getting close to your question—discover that certain concerns abroad,
due to pressures like shortages deliberately created by a foreign
power, are willing to pay fairly handsomely for harmless importation of simple capital equipment they need, well, frankly, I feel,
myself, I haven't too much complaint to make! I do not regard it as

scandalous to ensure machinery for industry—for perfectly harmless civilian repairs and replacements—to businessmen trying to run operations under such trying circumstances! I don't expect you two to understand what a nightmare it is to do business in sensitive countries—with or without inside political information! Your young friend Duane, now, was kind enough to quote me that line from Conrad you gave him about "secret agents of police" having unrewarding lives—rather an emotional term, I'd say—but let me just point out that I found many of these people to be gentlemen among gentlemen."

They were all quiet a moment. Then Francis thumped his manila envelope again. "What's in here," he said in a tone public speakers use, in obvious relief, when they can return to the subject after some idiotic question from the audience, "is a simple listing of the properties I am turning over to you and your sons. They are a perfectly predictable, ordinary spread of American interests. Gordy Landers made some of the suggestions, and I think they're very good. Burlington Industries, Con Edison, Telephone, Mac-Cabe and Janus, Ashland Oil, Wheeling Steel, First Bank Corporation, some Great Northern Iron Properties—that last ought to appeal, Bill—the holdings mostly right around here, I think." Francis added, "Now—do these sound like the work of the devil to you? They don't to me." He leaned back again, his cheeks and bloodless forehead gleaming.

It was most difficult to break into this manly, sensible-sounding monologue and say you didn't want your brother's money for you or your kids. All the time Bill talked his own voice sounded shaky and false to him, like the voice of Marchbanks. It sounded like a mixture of callow righteousness with callow unfamiliarity with "the world men have to live in, after all." He heard his own voice like a fool's voice, sailing on, in high, nervous timbre.

Then, marvelously quickly, he heard his wife's voice come on. In a daze, in a daze something like his feelings as a new bridegroom, he heard her voice begin without any pause after his own stopped: he heard Molly tell Francis that she felt exactly as Bill did. And all the time, on the surface of it, her voice, as his had, sounded portentous and stupid.

Then Francis was saying, "But you can't have talked this over! I only just told you about it!"

"All the rest is the same," Molly said. "You know that. We will take care of you. We are still standing by. That hasn't changed."

Francis said, "Well—that's good of you, Molly! Standing by! How easy the Prayer Book used to make it sound! The fact is, you don't know what dying is until it's your own dying." He gave a brisk laugh. "You had better take it from me, what a very special quality one's own dying has! I seem to have a very special feeling towards mine anyway!"

He got up now. "Nobody can say you two are chicken! It's not every day someone turns down a million and a half from his own brother or brother-in-law! And to his face, too! And without sleeping on it!" He went to the hall door and turned. "Now, some soft-headed types would have thanked a person and taken the gift in the spirit in which it was given, and knowing that the brother was on the way . . . *down*, as the kids say. These softheads might have felt they could afford to spare his feelings a little. They might have felt the guy'd been trying to serve the United States somehow, and now that he was dying he didn't have to have a bunch of someone else's assassinations and coups d'etat or whatever you two have on your mind laid at his feet! They could have given the money away to some goddamned left-wing charity later! But not you two! Not you two!"

From the pulpit next morning Bill wound up his sermon. He was saying, "What we have to consider on absolutely every occasion is, who's *invisible* in the scene?" As he spoke, he saw Duane Wolfmeyer creep into the back pew, pale with the gleam of a well-washed hangover. He decided to throw in an example just for Duane. Then he decided that was too vindictive. Then he changed his mind and did it anyway. "Even if we get paid just to change the towels every morning for an organization that is cruel, it still means" (he saw Duane listening with his left-over-prep-school manners) "we aren't keeping our invisible brother properly." Then Bill asked for their prayers "for Neil Wolfmeyer of this parish, and for the Whole State of Christ's Church."

In the choir room, priest and server helped each other lift off chasuble and surplice. Behind them, the people had just finished No. 346 and were waiting on their knees for LeRoy Beske to reappear in his red cassock and snuff the candles.

LeRoy said, "I changed serving with Brett Forsyth especially to serve with you this morning, Father."

His eyes were bright—not in admiration for the sermon, Bill decided.

"We made you this, Father. You got rid of the mouse roulette wheel, so we made this here." The boy handed over a piece of unusually clear birchbark. On it, a mouse was well drawn, in brown ink. The mouse looked up from its bark, its whiskers merged with the lines of the birch; its forefeet were slightly raised, dangling close together, its insubstantial jaw hung open, concentrating, the way mice do hang their jaws open. Bill thought it was the face of an animal that never, so long or so hard as it studied its enemy, could grasp how dangerous that enemy really is.

That morning Francis had borrowed the car and driven to Duluth to see his old friend Landers. All afternoon a few people hung about the lawns of St. Matthew's. They were dragging away the last of the bazaar gear. To everyone he came across, Bill showed the birchbark with the mouse on it.

Then, around dinnertime, he fell into a terrible mood. He told himself again how grateful he was that Molly and he had agreed on the only major material decision of their life together, but it didn't do any good. He was in a terrible mood. This was not a gentle mood of grief for his brother. It was a pure, bad mood.

He hunched past his study bookshelf and silently flung at Merton and Jeremy Taylor and John Donne, "Ah, easy enough to talk!" He went back outside and was rude to a perfectly nice Lutheran electrician who had put in hours sorting out the bazaar wiring and still wasn't through. He strode angrily across the beautiful lawn and didn't give a glance even to the lake. He thought: I'll never be seconded by anyone's state department to anyone's secret power group. No one who has any real say in who shall die and who shall live and what shall happen to any sizable portion of the earth's crust is ever going to turn to me in some sweaty meeting and say, "Damn it, Father—fill us in on the moral side of this thing, will you—are we okay?"

The priest flung himself into his house and dropped down beside the little boys in the living room. He read aloud to them a lot for the next two days. The boys clung to him on the Sears Roebuck couch. He kept reading everything over again instead of saying okay but this is the last time. He got up a falsetto for the witches' voices. He made the animals, when they spoke, howl and snarl and bellow twice as loudly as he ordinarily took pains to do. And as for the dragon, when it dragged itself up to the boulders where the princess was tied down, he gave out such resonant, such coarse and greedy hissing, the boys crowded against their father's middle-aged hips, and they pressed their heads against his shoulders.

The Dignity of Life

T WO PEOPLE STOOD QUARRELING in the Casket Showing Room. They were a sixty-three-year-old man named Marlyn Huutula and his unmarried sister Estona. She was so angry that she bent towards him from her end of the coffin.

"You really ought to keep your grimy hands out of that clean quilting!" Estona told him in a ferocious whisper. "As if you owned the place! As if Svea weren't lying dead this very minute, right here in this very building, and you showing no respect!"

Jack Canon, the funeral director, had been hovering near them. Now he gave a swift glance over to see how grimy Marlyn's hands were. He would let this grown brother and sister quarrel a moment; he meant to leave this end of the long Showing Room so that they would not feel self-conscious as they whispered furiously about prices.

Marlyn and Estona were buying a casket, and the service that went with it, for their aunt, Svea Istava, an old woman who had come down in the world. Svea had died alone in her wreck of a place just north of St. Aidan, Minnesota. From the time she moved there in 1943, until she died in February, 1982, she had always had a few faithful visitors. They would pick their way through her sordid front farmyard, avoiding the wet place and the coils of barbed wire. Her place was what was called "inconvenient": that is, it had no water up to the house. But whenever someone visited—Mrs. Friesman to leave her idiot son Momo, or Jack Canon, the funeral director, or on Sundays during the football seasons, her nephew, Marlyn Huutula—Svea filled their cups with smoky coffee.

Her most frequent visitor, Momo Friesman, found her dead. Next morning, people sitting around the Feral Café traded information about Svea, making her a kind of random liturgy. They told one another how Svea had taken better care of that dog, Biscuit, than she took of herself. They told each other it was certainly hard to believe that Svea Istava had ever been the wife of a Lieutenant Colonel in the 45th Field Artillery, whose body had not been sent home because that was during World War II, not Vietnam. Mrs. Friesman had seen his Bronze Star and his European Theatre of Operations ribbon bar hanging on cuphooks in Svea's smudgy cupboard. Finally, people in the café settled to the most interesting thing about Svea: they said she was worth $500,000. In one booth, the sheriff was talking about her to the state patrolman who lived in Marrow Lake. The Marrow Lake man went past Svea's place nearly every day and had never seen such a dump. But the sheriff said that you could tell the true class of a person, though, by how they treated a dog. He himself had a handsome white shepherd bitch; that Biscuit, now, originally was a runt from one of his litters. He had taken it over to Svea because he knew she would make it a good home, and so she had.

Everyone thought that Svea had left the whole $500,000 (if she had any $500,000) to her nephew Marlyn instead of half and half to Marlyn and his sister Estona. Marlyn visited her once a week for years, whereas Estona talked mean about Svea. Estona, who ran the Nu-St. Aidan Motel, was always roping in total strangers, finding out what they did, and then asking their advice. With both elbows on the sign-in counter, her eyes trying to read their bank balances when they opened their checkbooks, her wrists supporting her cheeks, she would say, "So you're a sales representative? As a sales representative, would you please tell me if this sounds right to you? I mean, you're in a position to know . . ." Then she would explain about Svea's money going to her kid brother because he was a man and made up to her on Sunday afternoons. Recently, she had said to the new Adult Education teacher who stayed at the motel on Wednesday nights, "You're a humanities consultant? Now that sounds like something that has got to be about how people treat each other! Fairly or unfairly? Well, would you tell me as a humanities consultant—would you call it fair that this old woman, who keeps her place so bad it is amazing they don't get the countryside nursing people in to spray around, do you think it is right she would leave all that money to my brother and not my half to me?" Estona regarded the humanities consultant as another middle-aged woman like herself, who had to have picked up some sense somewhere along the line. "I don't know if this is in your field or not, but just looking at it humanly, can you tell me that he is making any big sacrifices for his aunt when he can check on his Vikings and Steelers bets as good on Svea's eleven-inch black and white as he could on his own remote control at home? Or maybe it's just me."

As Marlyn and Estona stood around the Casket Showing Room, Jack Canon thought of everything that had happened since Svea's death. Her body had been discovered by Momo: Jack had quickly gone out to fetch it. He knew Momo as well as Svea, because Momo liked dead bodies. There was scarcely a wake or visitation in the past ten or fifteen years at which Jack hadn't had a word with Momo—that is, he had had to take him firmly by the elbow. Then, after he took Svea's body to the chapel, twenty or more youngsters went out to her place, apparently, and dug great holes all over the yard. By the time the sheriff reached the place, the boys had tipped over Svea's outhouse and were prodding the hole, looking for money. Another boy and girl had got hold of power augers and they were drilling into the frozen ground, like mining prospectors, among the stacked snowtreads and fence-wire wheels. The sheriff pulled them all in on Possession and Vandalism and then let them out again. He called Jack and said he was going to ask the state patrolman to help keep an eye open these next days. "If we are going to have any trouble," Jack told him, "it will be during visitation days, not at the funeral itself." The two men talked to each other quietly on the telephone, in the special, measured way of people holding the fort for decency and dignity—while all the others give in to some horrible craze. The sheriff said with a sigh, "Well, we'll manage! I've got to locate that nephew of hers now, wherever he is!" Jack felt the respect the sheriff had for him, a funeral director, and the disrespect he felt for Marlyn Huutula, who never had steady work in the wintertime if he could help it. Like half the men of St. Aidan, Marlyn kept a line of traps somewhere out east along St. Aidan Creek. Once he had tried to bribe the sheriff out of a speeding ticket while the sheriff stood at his car window, writing. Marlyn had picked up the rabbit lying on the passenger side and passed it up to the sheriff. The sheriff had been busy writing, so he didn't look carefully: all he saw was white fur and a little blood. At home, his shepherd had just had new litter of white puppies, so he mistook this animal. It was a full minute before he saw it was a rabbit, not a puppy. He had been writing a Warning; now he tore up the yellow card and gave the man a Cita-

tion instead. All day, as he later told Jack, his stomach churned.
Then he blushed. "I don't guess that would bother someone . . . in
your line of work," he added.

"Yes, it would bother him," Jack told him.

"I never had much tolerance," the sheriff said.

Jack Canon felt less tolerant every day now. He had started an
Adult Education course two weeks ago; he thought it would give
him perspective, but it was just the opposite. Now he minded remarks he heard that previously he would have passed off as "the
kinds of things people say."

He frequently thought of his crimson vinyl notebook that lay on
his office desk. It was labeled: HUMANITIES: ST. AIDAN ADULT EDUCA-
TION PROGRAM—MOLLY GALAN, INSTRUCTOR. Jack had never been a
man who took notes on his life as it went by. Yet now, several times
a day, he said to himself, sometimes even aloud, since he was a
good deal alone, "I ought to put *that* into the red notebook!" or
"*That* ought to go into the red notebook if nothing else ever does!"
And he looked forward to Wednesday night, the night of his class.

Tonight it was to meet in his office, as a matter of fact. That had
come about because two weeks ago, on Registration Night, only
one student had shown up to sign for the humanities course—Jack
himself. His teacher was a spare, graying woman with a white forehead, who was unlike anyone he had ever known. He glanced over
her head, her figure—her long hands with thin, unremarkable
fingers, trying to say "It is in the eyes," or "It is the hands," or "It is
how she *carries* herself"—but he knew all his guesses were wrong.
She leaned against the second-grade teacher's desk, and Jack sat
cramped before her in a desk-and-chair combination comfortable
only for small children. They waited for others to appear.
Through the schoolroom doorway, they heard shy voices, calls, remarks—people signing up for Beginning Knitting Two, a
continuation from the fall semester.

No one else came at all. Presently, Mrs. Galan explained that the
guidelines of the course would allow the class to meet in private
homes, if the class so chose. The following Wednesday, there was a
blizzard, but Mrs. Galan made it on I-35 from St. Paul to the Nu-St.
Aidan Motel, and to the schoolbuilding. This time she read off to
Jack some of the course subjects approved in the guidelines. They
might choose among Ethnicity, Sources of Community Wisdom,
Ethical Consciousness in Rural America, Longitudinal Studies of
Human Success and Failure, Attitudinal Changes Towards Death,

or simply Other. They agreed that the following Wednesday, since no one had shown up again this time, they might as well meet in Jack's office. He explained to her that she should walk round to the back of the chapel, where the back door opened onto a concrete apron. It was kept clear of snow, he told her.

In his years and years of single life Jack had noticed that lonely people were either carefully groomed or remarkably grimy. He himself had to be immaculate at all times. It was a habit by the time he was fourteen—along with learning how to cover the phone. He would push his arithmetic problems against the chapel schedule board, keeping the phone where his left hand could raise the earpiece on the first ring. Then he spoke immediately and courteously into the flared mouth. By the time he was a senior in high school he was used to nearly all the work of the chapel: he knew how to lift heavy weight without grunting, while wearing a white shirt, tie, and suit jacket. He learnt to keep longing or anxiety from showing on his face. One October day, in 1936, he was sitting on the football bench at St. Aidan High School. The big St. Aidan halfback sat down next to him, for just a minute. Jack had been sitting there, knees together, chilled, for an hour. The halfback, a great tall boy named Marlyn Huutula, dropped down beside him when he was taken out to rest a minute, and his body gave off heat and the glow of recently spent energy. It was nearly visible like a halo—that great hot energy field around the boy. Jack knew enough not to look at Marlyn for more than a second; he must not let himself be mesmerized into staring like a rabbit at a successful boy, the way he had seen others do. So Jack had given Marlyn a casual grin and both of them turned to watch the field. Then the coach snapped his fingers at Marlyn, who jumped up right in front of Jack. The coach's arm went around the leather-misshaped shoulders; Jack overheard the friendly growl of instructions. The coach pointed into the field with one hand, slapped Marlyn's buttocks with the other, and the halfback swung away towards the players, his socks sunk below his calves, jiggling in folds around the strong ankles. For the thousandth time that autumn, Jack expressed manhood by not letting his face look sad.

But the next Thursday afternoon, just as he was helping his father transfer a casket from the nervous pallbearers into the hearse, Jack recalled the bad moment on the football field. His face jerked upward in embarrassment at the memory. When his father had closed the hearse doors, he pulled Jack aside. St. Aidan Lutheran's

two bells kept tolling so the sound rang down nearly on top of
them: the sidewalk was white and cold with afternoon sunlight.
"I'm going to tell you this just once, but it is very important,"
Jack's dad said. "Do not put on a fake sad look—the way you did
just now when we were taking the casket. Get this straight: they
don't expect you to look sad—just professional. Just keep your
face serious and considerate."

Jack became more and more carefully gauged in his appearance:
he controlled his face, he maintained his grooming. But Svea
Istava, whose body now lay in his operating room, had turned
dirty as she aged. When Jack first knew her in 1943, she was a handsome woman of thirty-nine or so. She told him she had to give up
the St. Paul house that her husband's officer's pay had been fi-
nancing. She asked Jack if the World War II dead were going to be
returned to the United States. Next month, she bought an old, very
small farmhouse on an acre of scrubland, about a mile past St.
Aidan.

The first time Jack went out there to visit, his eye passed over the
turquoise-painted, fake-tile siding. He saw the string of barbed
wire that someone had hitched to one corner of the outhouse and
then stretched over to the cornerpost of the house itself. He supposed that Mrs. Istava would gradually have trash removed from
the farmyard. He hoped she would find enough money to put in
plumbing. He imagined the huge shade of the oaks darkening not
these piles of rejected auto batteries and other trash, but new lawn.
There was a distant view of both church spires, and to the north lay
the pleasant, spooky pine forest.

To his surprise, Svea didn't remove the barbed wire; she took to
leaning things against it—first a screen door that warped and she
couldn't repair, next a refrigerator that stopped working. Its rounded ivory corners and its rusted base grate seemed natural after a
while; Svea tied a clothesline length about it so that Momo Friesman would not climb inside and be killed. Sometimes she stood
the way poor rural people stand, elbow bent, one hand planted on
one irregular hip, and the face gazing vaguely past the immediate
farmyard, as if to say, "There is life beyond this paltry place—I
have my eyes on it."

In those days, Jack sometimes thought he would save Svea from
all that. He imagined himself, in a square-shouldered way driving
out one miserable winter night, when the sky would be black and
the ground-storming of down snow nearly blinding. "Oh, how

did you ever make it on such a night?" she would cry, and he would say briefly, a little sharply, "Come on—we're going to town! We're going to be married!" He imagined the reliable Willys pushing through all that darkness and whiteness.

It never happened. Svea never called a junk man to pick up anything in her yard. Instead, more junk arrived. Jack had to pick his way to the doorstep over corrugated-tread wheels of broken lawnmowers. Often, Momo stared at him from a pile of rubbish near the tipped refrigerator. He knew the child trapped mice and then buried them in a distracted, faithful way, among Svea's onion sets and carrots.

As the years passed, a rumor grew up that all this while Svea Istava had been and was still worth $500,000. The more unlikely her person and possessions, the more entrenched the myth.

Meanwhile, gradually, Jack began to lose confidence. He began buying more and more expensive clothing. By the 1960s, even his garden gloves were from L. L. Bean. He was the first man in St. Aidan to have a wool suit after a decade of Dacrons and polyester. By accident, he found out what was wrong with him. One evening, he sat with the sheriff down at the station. It had been a bitter February day, as it was now, and the sheriff was saying that the bad news in St. Aidan County was the rising crime rate but the good news was that more and more uranium leases were being let out around the area. Jack listened idly, leaning comfortably against the iron radiator, watching the heat move the window shades a little. The sheriff held several puppies on a pillow in his lap; his hands kept passing over the little dogs and the dogs kept rearranging themselves in a whining, growling, moving pile of one another. As Jack looked on, he felt that he was losing confidence because he wasn't touching other live bodies enough; he watched in an agony of envy as the puppies wandered with their fat paws into one another's eyes and ears and stomachs—he got the idea they were gaining confidence from one another every time they touched.

The next day he walked into the Feral Café to have lunch with the new Haven Funeral Supply salesman, Bud Menge. Haunted by the revelation of the puppies, he sensed that women looked up at Bud Menge as he went by, and rearranged their buttocks in the booths.

Bud was friendly, right from the first. After a year of their acquaintance, Jack said, "Couldn't you ever stop and let me buy you lunch without you trying to sell me something?"

Most dealing in St. Aidan took place at either the Men's Fellowship of St. Aidan Lutheran or at lunch in the Feral Café. Bud's face
grew grave and considerate. "Listen, Jack, how would you like to
discuss something that is absolutely new and different and will
revolutionize your whole approach?"

In ten minutes, Bud sold Jack an industrial-psychology program that he had used ever since. The Casket Showing Room
Lighting Plan, like all of Bud's ideas, was disgusting from the out-
set. "That's really revolting, Bud. Let's face it, Bud," he had said,
"That is just about the worst taste I have ever heard of!" Jack had
often made such remarks during Bud's first year as representative
for Haven Funeral Supply. Later he was slower to speak. Bud
never presented him an idea that was not absolutely profitable.

The first aspect of the Casket Showing Room Lighting Plan was
simple. You lighted only those caskets you wanted a client to in-
spect. You placed small wall-bracketed lamps at six-foot intervals
along the two long walls, and across one short end-wall of the
Showing Room. These lamps had either rose or cream shades: you
lit only those you wanted on each given occasion. Jack generally
lighted the caskets that went with the $1500 service, the $2300 service, and the $4000 service. No one in St. Aidan ever bought the
$4000 service, and in fact, it was not for sale.

This $4000 casket was an elaborate part of Bud's Lighting Plan.
Jack saw that it was lighted, and left its cover up, but did not lead
clients over to it. Bud explained the procedure: people shopping
for caskets feel that they are likely to be cheated by the mortician.
Even if the mortician is a fellow small-town citizen whom they
have known for years, they still feel they must watch him like a
hawk now that they are buying from him. They know perfectly
well that their own harrowed feelings at the time of a death are the
funeral director's pivot. They are on tiptoe against his solemnity.
Therefore, Bud explained, clients want to wander around the
Showing Room on their own: they feel they are getting around the
funeral director if they look at caskets besides the ones he seems to
want to show them. They want to be shrewd. Eventually, Bud explained, because it is lighted and open, the $4000 casket catches the
client's eye. He goes over, and, wonder of wonders, finds this casket
to be noticeably more elegant than anything the funeral director
has shown him so far. Immediately, he thinks that it is probably
priced the same as the caskets he has been shown, but simply is a
better buy. He suspects it is being kept for some preferred customer

of the funeral director, and that a comparative lemon is being pawned off on him at the same price. Bud told Jack, "You follow them over to the $4000 casket, but stay behind a little—as if you didn't really want to go over there. 'How come you never showed us *this* one?' they will ask. 'How come you never showed us this one when it's just beautiful?' they will say. So then you tell them, 'You're right—it is the most beautiful one, by far. It is the best casket we have ever had at Canon Chapel.' Just tell them that much at this point. Let them hang a little. Sooner or later the client will stop staring at you and will say, 'So how come you didn't show it to us?' Now here is where you pull your act together," Bud told Jack. "You tell them, fairly fast, 'Because I don't want you to buy that casket, is why.'" Bud begged Jack to pause again, right at that point. "Stick with the pauses, Jack, I'm telling you. Pause right there. Every single client—I don't care if it is the middle-aged mother of an only son who just died—every single client will say, 'But why don't you want me to buy it? What does it cost?' Now you go right up to the client and say, 'Because it costs $4000. I know you can afford $4000, Mrs. So-and-so, I know you can easily raise that amount. Money isn't the problem. The reason I don't want you to buy it is that I'd a hundred times rather that you bought the $2300 casket and gave the other $1700 to church or charity in memory of'—and you insert the deceased's name here—'I'd a hundred times rather you'd spent the $1700 extra that way than on a casket.' O.K., now, Jack, here is the third pause—don't make it very long—just a short one. Now you say, 'Or does that sound crazy, from where I'm supposed to be coming from?'"

Bud was right. No client ever said, "Yes, it sounds crazy." Men gave Jack a warm look and sometimes slapped his arm. Women sometimes came around the $4000 casket and hugged him. Everyone said, "Thanks, Jack, for being so square with us." And just as Bud had prophesied, not one of those clients ever bought the $1500 casket: they all bought the $2300 one. The whole point of the Lighting Plan was to switch people from the $1500 to the $2300 casket. During the whole sales procedure, Jack never had to lie. After explaining the Plan, Bud had paused briefly, then looked very straight at Jack across the strewn café booth table, with the chili bowls and paper sachets of coffee-whitening chemicals that both men had pushed away so they could lean forward on their forearms. "Some of them," Bud said, "I wouldn't bother to explain they don't have to lie—they wouldn't care. But with you, Jack, now that's a major thing."

The last point of the Casket Lighting Plan was to have one end of the Showing Room nearly dark. Jack made use of this point right now: he broke into the quarreling between Estona and Marlyn Huutula.

"Folks," Jack said loudly, "I am going to look over some odds and ends of paperwork. I'll be down at the other end of the room, so when you want me, give a call."

Clients needed the sense of quarreling privately. They needed to confer over how little they could spend without causing talk in town—talk about how cheap they were, after all that *he* or *she* had done for *them*, too. Jack always left people to have this quarrel, but he stayed within earshot so he could return at the right moment.

At a tiny writing table at the dark end of the room, just behind the county casket, Jack looked over an eight-page booklet showing full-color photographs of funeral customs all over the world. The photographs were on the right-hand pages, the "Discussion Questions" on the left-hand pages.

"What's the good of it?" Jack had said in the Feral Café, when Bud passed him the booklet across their coffee cups.

"It's the most practical thing we have come up with yet," Bud told him with his frank smile. "It solves the problem of the local necrophiliac. And every town has one."

Jack said, "I wish you wouldn't use that word in the Feral Café, Bud. In fact I wish you wouldn't use it at all. And besides," he added in the no-nonsense tone he used when he had to, his mind picturing Momo Friesman, "we haven't got anyone like that in St. Aidan."

"Every town has one," Bud said. "If you haven't got him today you will have him tomorrow. When some funeral director tells me his town don't have one, I look at the funeral director himself. Ha, ha! Just joking, Jack."

Bud opened the booklet to a page called *Funeral Practices of the Frehiti People*. "O.K.," he said. "Here's how it works. Your man shows up at a visitation or a wake."

"And who are the Frehiti People? What do we care!" said Jack.

Bud grinned. "How should I know who they are? They don't live around here anyway. Anyway, they're somebody. Some sociologists or humanities people or somebody did all the research—we know it's O.K. That's a point I'm glad you asked about, Jack. You know, the research in this booklet didn't come from our publicity department like most of the stuff. This is the real thing—you can be confident when you use this. Anyway, your guy comes up at the wake so you go up to him and you put your arm around his shoulder, the nice, teaching way a football coach throws his arm around you and you feel good because you know the coach is taking you into his confidence. O.K? Didn't you say you played football for St. Aidan High? O.K.—then you know the way I mean. Now, with your free hand, Jack, you flip open this booklet. It is easy because they put this Frehiti People discussion at the center where the stapling is, so it naturally opens right there. So you keep your other hand on his shoulder, see, and you show him this picture, the one you see there, with the jungle huts in the background, and them carrying the corpse in a kind of thatch-covered chair with the feet hanging off like that, towards us. And the Discussion Questions at the left. So you don't have to tell this person, 'Look at the terrific picture of a dead body with the feet hanging off that kind of coolie chair or whatever it is.' What you get to say aloud is, 'I wonder, so-and-so—you want to use their name as much as you can, Jack, as you know—'Hey, so-and-so, I wonder if you'd look through this new book and read these Discussion Questions. Maybe this is something that would help families get through grief—would you look this over and then tell me what you think?' And Jack, all the time you are saying all this, his eyes are glued onto that picture and his mind is thinking, if people like that think, There are other full-color pictures in the book, too, and I want to see them all! Then he hears you offering to let him take the booklet home with him. Now all this time, you are pushing him along right out of your funeral chapel and he is halfway home before he realizes he is no longer at the visitation. And that is fine with you. The last thing you need is someone trying any sensitivity games at a visitation."

Bud gestured toward the booklet in Jack's hand. "That little item may not have a lot of class like our bronze desk accessories and all, but it is one hundred thousand percent effective."

Now Jack sat at the dark end of the Showing Room, looking at the dead Frehiti in the photograph. The man's feet, whitened in the foreground, in sharp focus, were separated from the gloomy jungle village in the background; the feet had come to meet the viewer; the straw hut roofs, the gnarled equatorial trees, the smudgy broken grass of the village street—all that receded and lowered behind, like a cloud departing.

Jack heard Estona Huutula's voice rise in fury. He was used to family differences in his Showing Room, but this one was especially nasty. He listened, trying to decide when he should break in.

"I don't see how you can be so uncaring," Estona was shouting. "You know that when they open up that will, there will be a half million for you—probably for you, alone, too; you won't even have to share it with me, since you did such a good job making up to Svea all those years! You know what people will say, Marlyn! They'll say that there that nice aunt left him a cool half million and all he would buy her was the county casket."

"I never said I wanted to bury Svea in the county casket!" Marlyn shouted back.

The casket they referred to was a narrow, light blue coffin that St. Aidan provided for welfare clients when the family could afford nothing else. It was nicely made, but most funeral directors, including Jack, made sure it was locally referred to only as "the county casket" so that no one would contemplate buying it for a loved one.

"All I meant was," Marlyn said, "why go to $2300 when we can get the same service and a perfectly nice-looking casket for $1500?"

Jack rose from his small desk.

Estona said, "That's going to look just fine, isn't it, when you get all that money? I call it downright cheap!"

Marlyn grumbled, "We don't even know if Svea had any money anyway."

"All the worse for you then!" cried Estona with a slashing laugh. "All those Sunday afternoons you put in for nothing! Sitting there in her filthy kitchen letting her tell you how Chuck Noll should do this, Chuck Noll should do that, and how old age comes even to football players, and how Cliff Stoudt was a fool to hurt his arm. That one time I was there, you must have said it twenty times if you said it once: 'You may have something there, Svea!' I nearly puked. And 'Everything that goes up has to come down, I guess, Svea— even Lynn Swann!' If you weren't the sponging wise nephew of the sports-expert aunt! And the two of you drunk as lords before three in the afternoon, too! I nearly threw up listening to you—I'd say 'puke' except we're in a funeral chapel!"

Jack generally let relations quarrel until both of them had turned their irritation, by mere exhaustion, from each other to him. As soon as he felt all the anger coming towards him—none left for each other—he would spend a minute deliberately hardselling a coffin he knew they didn't want. Then they would concentrate on outwitting this awful funeral director for a minute or so. He let them outwit him. Then he decided which coffin they would really like, and usually wrapped up the sale, including choice of Remembrance folders, in fifteen minutes. The clients left in harmony with each other, which was good: the moment they left Canon Chapel the elation of having stumped the mortician would die and they would notice and carry their grief again.

"And another thing!" Estona cried. "You know, if you had *really* respected Svea's dignity in life or death, you wouldn't have been out tomcatting the very night after they found her, would you? There we were, the sheriff and I, trying to figure out where you were, with all those kids having dug up poor Svea's yard and all! Do you know that the sheriff sent the deputy down the river because they thought you were checking your traps? Finally Mrs. Friesman said she seen you driving somewhere with that Mrs. Galan from the Adult Education. 'Oh,' I said, 'he wouldn't be with her. She always stays with us at the Nu-St. Aidan Motel.' Well, yes, she saw you though, she said, so what could the sheriff do; he drove back out to your house and there you were in the middle of the night, the both of you! Of course I'd made a fool of myself, telling the deputy I knew you wouldn't be running around with her because she seemed like such a nice widow lady and very intellectual."

Jack now made his way slowly from the dark end of the room, like someone a little off balance. He approached the brother and sister standing under the yellow wall lights and took Estona by the elbow. He explained that they would now go into his office and have a sip of something that he kept, which sometimes helped people in times of grief. He led them around behind the chapel, past the door leading to the operating area, and into his office. Sunlight poured in, dazzling after the draped and shadowy Showing Room. Jack seated Estona on the couch; he put Marlyn in the conference chair, and opened a bottle of Pinot Blanc. Although everyone in St. Aidan knew that Estona Huutula turned on the NO part of the NO VACANCY sign at the motel each night around ten, and settled down with a whiskey, Estona said, "I don't use much alcohol, Jack, but a little wine *would* help me, I think."

Estona then allowed they ought to get the $2300 white-lined casket instead of the $1500 tan-lined one because it would be more cheerful for Svea to look out of. Both men looked out through the faint window curtains when she said that. She added, "Or maybe that's just me."

In the normal course of things, Jack would have let Estona sell
Marlyn on the more expensive of the two caskets, but now he wanted this old high school classmate and his sister out of the office so
badly he would have sold him a co-op burial-club service with a
pine box for $34.50 if they would just get out. So he took it into his
own hands. Ignoring Estona, who was tapping her glass for a re-
fill, he spoke to Marlyn in a man-to-man tone, making fast ex-
planations. He filled the man in on some of the side services provided in a funeral, such as getting police cooperation in case there
was further trouble, or unwanted crowds to see the body of a simple old woman worth $500,000. He explained that his own man,
LeVern Holpe, would park cars, assisted by the chapel man from
Marrow Lake.

Marlyn responded exactly as Jack wanted: he tried to be snappy
and intelligent too. Marlyn never mentioned the $1500 casket
again. Then, just when Estona was beginning to look as if she felt
neglected, Jack passed her the new Remembrance format that Bud
Menge had brought over only the week before. Gone was the
Twenty-third Psalm in Old English eleven point on the left-hand
side: instead, there was a passage from *The Velveteen Rabbit* in a
modern face without serif. Jack said to Estona, cutting Marlyn out
of it: "Estona, I want your honest opinion of these. If you don't
care for these new-style Remembrances, say so, and we will have
the others printed up for Svea."

At last brother and sister were gone. Jack telephoned LeVern to
say that he could come over and work any time now. He himself
would have a catnap. He lay down on the small office sofa.

The winter sun, very bright and low at this time of year, sent its
long webby light through the glass curtains. Jack fell gratefully
asleep, still wearing his suit jacket. Sunlight fell onto his desk with
all the accessories Bud had provided him—the bronze-tone plastic
paperweight imprinted CANON CHAPEL: CARE WHEN CARE MATTERS
MOST. The sun fell onto his red-covered humanities notebook, too.
It fell onto his own face, and made his white hair nearly transparent
and his skin luminous. Once during the following hour and a
half, his young assistant, LeVern, looked in soundlessly and thought
how sad the human face looks asleep; he decided that Jack Canon,
in his opinion anyway, led a very crappy life. LeVern decided he
could manage the job without waking the fellow, and called Greta
at the beauty parlor when he was done to tell her she could come

over and do Mrs. Istava's head now or whenever she was ready.

In his dream, Jack went to spend the weekend in a motel north of St. Paul. He was to meet a woman there who had exclaimed, "My God! I think I am falling in love again! I love you, John!" So long as Jack still believed she would show up, he patrolled the motel room, swerving round the ocean-sized bed and rounding the television set like an animal. Once he had decided she was not going to show up, he took to rereading all the materials in the desk except the Bible placed there by the Gideons. Everything he read swam and enlarged and darkened in his eyes. Everything had color swimming at the edges; even the papers he held were yellowed like church windows on Christmas cards. He read through the Room Service Menu with its appalling prices and his eyes swam with tears. He read the Daily Cleaning Services options with his eyes silvered with tears. He was reminded of something that someone at a Minnesota Funeral Directors' convention had once told him: the man had said that when he became Born Again, for the first few weeks, whenever he opened up the Bible, no matter at what place he opened it, his eyes would fill with tears. Jack was thinking that over, in his dream, when he waked to LeVern's tapping on the office door.

LeVern put his head around the door. "All set now, Jack," he said. "I'm going home now."

"Oh, then, you're ready for me," Jack said, trying not to sound slowed with sleep.

"No, it's all done," LeVern told him. "Greta's here working now."

Jack lay vulnerable in the huge sadness of his dream. The day was nearly over. All morning he had longed for the day to be over, because it was Wednesday, the night of his class. Now the joy was gone out of it.

Eventually, he rose and bathed and shaved and put on the best sports jacket he had. He looked at his gray eyes very carefully in the mirror, but it was O.K.: none of the dream or his own feelings showed.

He locked the front door of the chapel, making sure the twin lights for visitations were both turned off; people understood by that that Svea could not be viewed until the next day. Then he went round and lighted the rear yard light, which fell upon the private entrance to his office and the garage. At nearly eight o'clock, the bell rang. Jack cried to himself, "She came after all, then!"

He swung the door open to the cold night. Outside, Momo Friesman stood on the garage cement, his bulging eyes bright from the
overhead light.

"I came to pay my respects to Mrs. Istava," Momo said quickly,
"and don't you turn me away, Jack. I got a right. She was neighbor
to me, and my mother and I was friends. She had me come keep her
company once a week and I got a right to mourn her as good as
anyone else."

"Visitation isn't until tomorrow, Momo," Jack said.

Then he recalled Bud Menge's little book of photographs and
discussions. "There *is* something you could help me with, though,
Momo. Do you have time to come in a minute?"

Momo's eyes shone. "I can help you in the lab, Jack!"

"No," Jack said firmly, "not in the operating room—but wait."
He started to go to the Casket Showing Room for the booklet, but
then remembered he couldn't leave Momo alone or the man might
leap through the office door towards the operating room. So he
put his arm around Momo's shoulder and led him to the sofa.
When he saw Momo was all the way seated, he left.

Momo had the face of a twelve-year-old; he was forty-three, in
fact. Every morning in the summer, his mother drove him into
town and Momo went to all the trash disposal cans in St. Aidan,
recovered *Minneapolis Tribunes* from them, and sold them up and
down the one street of the town, shouting, "Paper! Paper!" All the
business people sent someone out, a receptionist or whoever was
nearest the door, to give Momo a nickel and take a paper. When he
had gone the whole length of the street, from the Canon Funeral
Chapel at one end to the Rocky Mountains Prospectors' office at
the other, he would find more papers lying on top of the trash cans,
so he sold them again—this time to the other side of the street. At
noon he waited among the boxes that came into the Red Owl on
the truck; the owner would shout, "He's here, O.K., Mrs. Friesman!" when his mother came to pick him up. Once a week she
took him over to Svea Istava's place across the road, and Svea
would let him dig in her piles of orange crates and used winter tires.

When Jack dropped the booklet into Momo's lap, it opened as
Bud had promised, to the photograph of the dead Frehiti man in
his grassy chair. Jack thought to himself, "It is eight-oh-five now.
She hasn't shown up. She is not going to come. Well," he went on
to himself, "everyone has to have some kind of memorial made in

their honor. We shouldn't any of us die without someone's doing at least *something* in our honor." Jack looked down at Momo, who was bent over the photograph. "Well, Momo," Jack thought, "you're it. Svea let you into her place all those years. Tonight, then, I will let you into mine. You can sit there and gloat over that book for two hours if you want." Jack went and sat down at his desk. He said in his thoughts, "I don't suppose you'd understand, Momo, if I tried to explain to you that Molly Galan was supposed to be sitting here where you are sitting, not you. Well, anyway—it isn't her: it's you." Jack remembered how Svea remained kind to Momo even when, two weeks after her dog Biscuit died, Momo found the grave, despite the rusty refrigerator grille Svea had laid on top of it in hopes he wouldn't notice. Momo dug up Biscuit and brought the body into the house and laid it on Svea's oilcloth-covered table. Biscuit looked bad after two weeks in the earth. Even then, Svea did not lift a hand to Momo. She only telephoned Jack to ask if he ever had had any difficulty with Momo around the chapel. Jack confessed that he had to deal with Momo on various occasions.

Now he went through the little speech Bud had taught him, suggesting Momo take the booklet home. He need not have bothered. Just as Bud predicted, Momo was entranced by the pictures.

The doorbell rang again.

Jack went over to it, nearly faint with hope but still unbelieving.

"I didn't know if I ought to come," Molly Galan said. "I know you have had a death."

"Oh, but visiting isn't until tomorrow!" Jack cried. He held the door wide, but didn't offer his arm. Molly Galan explained that she was a little breathless from having walked over from the motel. Then Jack remembered Momo. "This is Momo Friesman," Jack said. He went over and stood near Momo's knees. "Momo is going to zip up his jacket now and take his book home, before it gets even later and colder."

"I want to stay here," Momo said.

"Let's see your book," Molly said.

"You give that back," he told her.

"I promise," she said. She sat down beside him, turning the pages.

"And now you must take it home with you, Momo," Jack said. "But first you must zip up your jacket because it is much colder again now."

Jack realized that in one minute Momo would be out of there, and the thought made him so joyous he nearly danced the man into his zipper.

"I don't want to go," Momo said.

Jack thought, "I could just strangle him until those eyes jump clear out of his head like twin pale spheres careening out into space and then I could pick him up and throw the whole mess of a man out the door." As soon as Jack noticed what he was thinking he backed further from the sofa. Anyway, he thought, retreating to the desk, what did he care if Momo chose to stay the evening? What good would it do *now* to have an evening with Molly Galan?

"Oh yes!" he cried to himself. "Look at that flushed face of hers! And that lively look in her eyes: that isn't from hiking over here in the cold! And her wonderful smile!" That smile was turned towards Momo, but how could such a smile be for Momo? Women of fifty did not look like that except when love was so recent the body itself still remembered it. Jack's anger narrowed and cooled and felt permanent. "And anyway," he added to himself, "all this is just a job of work for a woman like her." She was hired to tutor adult extension students in the humanities, so she tutored adult extension students in the humanities. She had agreed to meet in his office probably because that arrangement was simpler than anything else.

He said aloud, "Well, if Momo wants to stay, that would be all right, wouldn't it?"

She looked at Momo and said, "Of course. Momo, you can read your book and we will work on ours."

"And afterwards I will pay my respects to Svea," Momo told her.

"Not tonight," she said. "When I say it's time you will zipper up your jacket and you can walk home with me."

In the meantime, Jack walked rapidly back and forth between his lighted desk and the sofa. Perhaps Molly Galan was going to open her copy of the red humanities workbook over there, on the sofa beside Momo. She might do that, he supposed.

But she didn't. She came to his desk and sat down in the conference chair. She picked up a bronze marker stamped CANON CHAPEL and laid it back quickly. She said, "The Extension people would like to know which subject we're going to work on. And they want us to write an evaluation as we go along. This is a kind of pilot program, you see." She smiled at him. "They want to know what your expectations are."

How could Jack tell her his expectations? All week he had

planned how she was coming and he meant to tell her part of his life story. Shamelessly, he had meant to. Jack had meant to tell her how all his life he had wished to be serious, not just solemn as he must be at his work, but serious. He wanted to tell her how here in St. Aidan, where he practiced a trade he had never wanted to practice, somehow he could not rise over the chaff and small cries of daily life into some upper ring of seriousness. He imagined this ring of seriousness, like Saturn's rings, almost physically circling the planet—but he couldn't reach it because he was caught down here, blinded in the ground-storming of old jokes, old ideas, old conventions, which no sooner were dropped than they were picked up again like snow lifted and lifted and dropped and lifted again by blizzard wind, blowing into everyone's face over and over.

Molly Galan smiled at him. She had placed the four fingers of her right hand between five pages of the humanities notebook, and she held these pages apart as if for ready reference; he saw the lamplight through the spread pages like a nearly translucent Eastern fan, collapsible, of course, but taking up its space as elegantly as sculpture does.

Jack thought, How can it be that anyone with such hands spent last night with Marlyn Huutula? How can that be, when Marlyn Huutula all his life had never done anything admirable except play halfback for St. Aidan in 1936?—and Jack saw, as sharply in his mind's eye as he had ever seen it, Marlyn's sweaty hair as he removed his leather helmet.

Now Jack bent towards Molly under the beautiful lamplight and shouted at her, "What I want to know is, why did you ever do it? How could someone like you go and, go and, oh how could someone like you for the love of God go and spend the night with Marlyn Huutula? How could you *do* it?"

"I know I did not just say that aloud," Jack told himself; "I know I did not. Nonetheless, that is what I just did. However, I must not have really said that aloud because men in their sixties do not ask humanities consultants why they spend the night with whomever they spend the night with. Yet it was my voice that said that."

Then he thought: "In one minute she will simply rise and leave without another word. She will go over to the couch and pick up her coat where she left it near Momo and she will leave. I shall offer her a ride home because it is so cold again and, oh, Christ, she will refuse even that!"

However, the ladylike fingers did not fold up the fan. Molly Galan shouted at him, "I don't know! I don't know why I did it! And what do *you* care, anyway?"

"I don't care! I don't care what you do," Jack said.

"Well," Molly shouted, "you just don't know how dumb it all is!"

She burst into tears.

Very far inside himself, in a place really too dank to nourish a spark of happiness, Jack felt a tiny warmth: "What do you mean, 'dumb'?" he asked. But then the snarl came back into his voice. "So what's that supposed to mean, *dumb!* What is that supposed to mean, 'How dumb it all is!' Anyone can go around shouting things like that!"

"You don't know what it is to be lost in the dumbness of it!" she shouted, still crying.

"You chose it! You chose it!" he said. "You chose Marlyn Huutula!"

Suddenly then her hands fell simply, faintingly, like snow onto the booklet in her lap. Her face and voice suddenly were completely serene. "Yes," she said, pausing. "That's right," she said in an agreeable, logical tone. "Marlyn Huutula. Now he really *is* dumb." She added in an even more peaceful tone, "That is a fact, you know. He is really *very* dumb."

"The dumbest person I ever knew!" Jack said. But then he leaned forward and said, "What do you mean exactly?"

He felt a hope taking fire in him too quickly. He did not want to lose his proper anger in this hope. Already, he noticed that Molly was sitting with her head tipped to one side, nearly daydreaming at him, and he, too, on his side of the lamplight, was tipping his head at the same angle. They regarded each other like two birds, with that great concentration and that great natural stupidity of birds.

Hope kept rising rather weakly in Jack, like a hand rising from a lap, with the fingers still fallen from the rising wrist, the fingers flowing downward like an umbrella.

Momo meanwhile had approached them, and now wavered, his face turning from one to the other of them.

Jack whispered, "Well, will we go on with the course, do you think?"

Molly said, "Of course we will."

Jack said briskly. "It is too cold for you and Momo to walk

home. I will drive you both. Momo, it is time for you to zip up your jacket now."

The telephone rang. It was the sheriff. "Jack, I thought you would like to know. The Huutula family read Svea Istava's will early, and you know what? She didn't have two cents to her name! After all that fuss! So what we'll do, Jack—the Marrow Lake patrolman and I will kind of keep an eye out the next couple of days, and we'll make sure the news gets around, so you shouldn't have any crowd-draw to the visitation hours. I expect you'll just get the usual for an old woman like that." In the background, Jack could hear the sheriff's puppies barking.

Jack and Momo and Molly all sat in the front seat of his car. The night had dropped below zero, so their breathing frosted the windshield and the side windows as well. The defroster opened up only a small space in the windshield directly in front of Jack; he had to hunch down to see through it. He guided the car gingerly through the cold town out on the north road towards the Friesmans'. The black woods were not wrecked, but they were nearly wrecked. The greater trees had been cut over. The earth under the forest was not wrecked, either—but it was staked out. Here and there, invisible to ordinary people, were concrete-stoppered holes where the uranium prospectors had pulled out their pipes and left only magnets so they could find the places again. As the car crawled along the iced highway, Jack thought of the whole countryside, nearly with tears in his eyes. He kept peering through the dark, clear part of the glass, with his whole body shivering and his skin cold in his gloves and the whole of him beginning to flood with happiness. His own life, Jack thought—it wasn't wrecked completely, after all! It felt to him, since he was sixty-three and much was over for him—or rather, had gone untravelled—that his life was nearly wrecked. But not completely. He began to smile behind his cold skin. He started driving faster, feeling more jaunty and more terrific every second.

The patrolman from Marrow Lake, who had just left the St. Aidan station, happened to see the car tearing along Old 61 where it crossed the north road. He thought, "Oh, boy! Travellers' advisory or no travellers' advisory! Nothing stops some people! Car all frosted blind like that, tearing right along anyway!" Behind the car's pure white windows he did not make out the local undertaker and a comely woman and a middle-aged retarded man.

Talk of Heroes

TWO WOMEN, one with hair gone gray, wearing a woolen dress and carrying a raincoat, and the other only twenty-four, gathering the velvet lapels of her dressing gown around her throat, stood a moment on a low hill overlooking White Bear Lake. A thick evening mist lolled upward from the lake surface itself, so that all the dockside equipment—the polyurethane floats, the white boat lifts, the bobbing milk cartons chained to great weights far below—all the bright playthings of American Midwest lakefronts were hidden. The evening mist suggested much greater, more classic waters than a suburban lake.

Emily Anderson had meant to pause alone for a second before jumping into her car and driving to St. Paul to introduce a speaker, but her daughter, Sandra Anderson-Keefer, had ambled out of the house after her. Sandra began to tell an odd dream she had had when she fell asleep in the late afternoon. It was not exactly to do with Bruce, her husband, but somehow she felt it had to do with a vague semblance of him. Not like a ghost exactly, she told Emily, but something unclear and generalized. Emily shifted the raincoat on her arm and started energetically across the cold grass for the car, with Sandra following, trying to explain the dream sequence.

Emily was feeling the elation of conscientious hosts when they can temporarily escape a ubiquitous houseguest. No matter that Sandra was her daughter, and a humorous and kindly-inclined girl, home to get it, as she put it, all together for a few days—the fact was, Sandra talked a lot and Emily wasn't used to it.

She had not yet given up the silent house on its rise over the lake, the oak trees' dripping, the autumn fogs in the morning and evening. She was used to standing outside for her early morning coffee. She was used to moving about her work, from room to room, without conversation. In the past four days, however, Sandra had

followed her from her book-packing in the library to her cleaning
of the downstairs closets. Sandra generally left her alone when she
made off to her study, saying, "Oh—you're going to work! I won't
invade," and wandered into the living room for an afternoon nap.
Like many people in personal turmoil, she rose late, didn't dress
other than to cloak herself in her dressing gown, and she fell asleep
easily throughout the day. For a few hours, late after dinner, she
would talk in a jerking, high-pitched voice, about her married life.
Her young face gleaming nervously, she would repeat for Emily
what Bruce, her husband, had said and then what she had replied.
She was trained as a group therapist, so she tended to use phrases
like "thinking through her options"—but the griefs of men and
women, getting along, not getting along, were there, recognizable
despite her sporty jargon.

Emily hid her own relief at escaping for an evening by crying
once more as they neared the car, "You're absolutely sure you don't
want to come with me to the Tusend Hjem program? Old Mr.
Elvekrog—poor dear—would be happy to see you! He'd welcome
any member your age—probably with open arms!"

"I bet!" Sandra said.

"And wasn't Chuck Iversen an old friend of yours? He still
comes, for his dad's sake no doubt—but he does try to brighten
things up."

Sandra said with a laugh, "I made the Tusend Hjem scene with
you and Dad for fifteen, sixteen years, and it ruined one evening of
every single Christmas vacation, too! Don't you try to talk me into
it, Mama! I couldn't hoke up the slightest enthusiasm in Norwegian-
American culture now if you gave me a million dollars." Sandra
paused. "Seriously, Mama—if you were the speaker you know I
wouldn't miss it for anything! But you're introducing—so what
we're looking at is a first-quality, four-minute introduction and
then a half-hour of horrible speech and a half-hour of horrible
slideshow . . . ."

"Movie!" said Emily laughing.

"Horrible movie, complete instructions in how to knit Norwegian socks! Then another horrible hour of cookies and coffee
with enough caffeine and sugar intake to o.d. Norway itself for a
week! And then the awful singing of the Norwegian national anthem, with everyone pretending they still understand the words
and care two cents for what they mean! No, Mama—sorry! I think

you're awfully good to do it, but Tusend Hjem is definitely not one
of my priorities."

Emily gave her briefcase a cheerful toss into the back seat. "The
movie isn't Norwegian knitting," she said. "That's what they were
going to have—Mrs. Thorstad talking about Norwegian knitting.
But apparently the national office in Brooklyn called up and
changed the program. The movie is about World War II."

"Oh my God," Sandra said, smiling in through the open car
window. "But I can see why you're interested. You and Dad knew
someone, whoever it was, who was in it, didn't you? But it's not my
war, Mama. And I know too much about human relationships
now to pretend to have feelings I haven't got." She added, with a
small lift of chin, "I have kind of a sense of my own war, sort of."

Emily told her, "I will be back as fast as I can leave."

Sandra looked chilled and uncertain; her dressing gown at this
late time of day suggested a patient in a hospital rather than a
grown woman trying with any bravado to decide whether or not to
leave a husband. Emily felt sorry for her, but also at odds: her own
mood was public and practical. She was geared simply to do a job.
Sandra was thinking of passion only, wandering through her own
personal situation all these days. Emily felt the superior edge of ad-
ministrators who feel superior to expressive talkers—simply because the talkers happen not to be doing any particular work at the
moment.

She drove gladly into the gloomy evening. It was only twenty
minutes into St. Paul, to West Seventh Street, where Tusend Hjem
leased the entire upper story of a very old, well-made brick building. Tusend Hjem was chartered in 1897 as the Minnesota chapter
of the national organization of Norwegian-American immigrants.
In the old days, there had been tri-weekly gymnastics classes, and
everyone had spoken Norwegian, and had known the anthem
from which the name, *tusend hjem*, or thousand homes, was
taken.

Even now, Mr. Elvekrog's program committee made sure there
was a meeting once a month, with some sort of cultural offering.
And even when the program content itself left something to be
desired (like the films occasionally sent out from the national office), the people could still count on the Norwegian-style boiled
coffee, brought up three times with an egg—and the homemade

cookies. Mrs. Iversen's committee kept the great gloomy hall absolutely clean; the chipped tiles in the kitchen and bathrooms were scrubbed regularly. Everyone wished they could reach the great west window to wash it.

It was a huge Roman arch, with radiating pie-sections of glass and blackened lead-soldering. It looked like a window meant to light genuinely serious human affairs, like the window of an old science laboratory where honest discoveries were made, or the window of a major embassy where people argued late at night about affairs later described in the papers. In the summertime the sun would just be failing as Tusend Hjem started its meetings, and a smeary, kindly light fell through the dusty glass arch, showing the gym ropes still knotted neatly and the rows of auditorium chairs. Along the high, plastered walls hung photographs of 1920s and 1930s gym classes; the men's knees, jutted out toward the photographer, must by now be full of creaks and aches, if not in many cases put to rest.

Emily closed the heavy street-door of the building, with its clanking nightchains. She started up the clean, wooden stairs. Above her head, she heard the committee members scurrying between kitchen and the great hall. They would be unpacking nine-by-seventeen trays of chocolate bars and paper plates of krullers and fattigmenn, in their little prisons of Saranwrap. The women did not let the men simply stand around, either. "Here—you, Merv!" Mrs. Thorstad cried, just as Emily came to the landing, "Take this!" Then, Mrs. Iversen, hearing Mrs. Thorstad's remark, looked about for her Chuck. He was lounging under a framed illustrated print of the Lord's Prayer in Norwegian, joking with Bernt Nielsen. "You can make yourself useful, too!" his mother cried. "They'll be coming in another fifteen minutes now!" Chuck Iversen was regarded as the clown of Tusend Hjem, so now he made some witty rejoinder and then caught sight of Emily. "O boy!" he shouted, laughing, at her. "Good thing you got here!" He began separating dozens of styrofoam coffee cups. "Old Elvekrog is climbing the walls in there worrying—'Will Emily show up O.K.?' he asks everyone!"

Emily said with a smile, "He knows perfectly well I'll show up."

Chuck told her, "Yes, but he doesn't know about that so-called famous speaker from Norway that's coming—the one you're supposed to introduce!" Chuck waved his head back to a partitioned corner of the hall. It was an eight-foot-high enclosure, making a little office, something like the little offices put into great factory spaces—islands isolated off from the general noise and work. "You'd better go in there and cheer him up," Chuck said.

Mr. Elvekrog leapt up from his seat the moment she went in the doorway of his office. He came round the desk to give her a brief, limp handshake. "Sometimes I just don't know what to do about National!" he cried.

"What have they done?" Emily asked. She sat down with her raincoat in her lap. Above the flimsy plywood and two-by-four construction of the office, she could see the huge ceiling of the main hall, and part of the steel and glass window. Immediately next to her was a little table covered with thick, artificial velvet of silver-green: on it, in a neat semi-circle, stood propped-up small photographs of Ibsen, Björnstjerne Björnsen, Hamsun, and Haakon VII. There was also a very bright Kodacolor picture of fourteen or fifteen middle-aged American women stuffed into Hardanger national costumes. Their permanents and wing-shaped eyeglasses were heart-breaking, over the blouses of openwork embroidery. Opposite the table stood a file case in which all Tusend Hjem members had file folders. As they died, their folders were moved from the upper drawer to the lower one. Last August, when Emily's husband's file was moved, Mr. Elvekrog had kindly sent her the ribbon awarded her husband for fifty years of Tusend Hjem membership.

Now Mr. Elvekrog, looking very old and nervous, said, "Well! I wanted to talk to you in here—but of course it doesn't give much privacy!"

Everyone who passed the office looked in. Women went by with Mason jars in which orange sticks bearing tiny Norwegian flags were arranged in a circle, with some Kleenex stuffed in the center to keep them in position. Chuck Iversen and Bernt Nielsen passed, listening to Mrs. Thorstad, who was talking loudly about knitting.

"National needn't act so high-handed with me!" said Mr. Elvekrog. "They aren't such fine folk! I was there once, Emily—I wonder if I told you? Right in their office, there, at National. Their office—now—why, it's not even in New York City. It's in Brooklyn and I had a terrible time just to find the place. You have to know to take the BMT subway to the Forty-Sixth Street stop. But Emily—I don't have to tell you—you and your husband must have been there, when you went through on your way to Norway that time, at least! The time I was there, I had called ahead to say I was coming—but do you think anyone met me? Not a soul! All there was was a janitor is all, someone just hired, too—not a genuine Tusend Hjem volunteer—not a real member. And this janitor kept vacuuming around my feet. I kept thinking that the hired coordinator—that's the kind of things they go in for these days—a hired coordinator—would come greet me. Finally, the janitor said, would I move my feet. That did it, Emily! I told him straight out, 'You bet I will! I will just move them right out of here, too!' I have always wondered if the janitor told the rest of them how quick I talked right up to him! Emily, when they call you from National, you would think they were calling from the gates of heaven for the tone they put on! This hired coordinator that called two weeks ago, she made me cancel the evening we had all planned for tonight—all because of this famous Norwegian war hero who was doing a tour across the country anyway!"

"Willi Varig," Emily said.

"Yes, this Willi Varig," Mr. Elvekrog said. He went on in his bitter tone: "I had already asked Mrs. Thorstad would she do her knitting patterns for us. You see, for all these past six weeks we have had an announcement up that Mrs. Thorstad would be showing us the Norwegian knitting patterns which she brought back from Bergen last summer. In the original Norwegian language, too, but with her own translations into English measure. And afterwards, Mrs. Iversen was going to serve her homemade krullers. I try to keep that bulletin board up to date, you know—and then suddenly, National calls up and says we have to have this war hero. Well, Emily—in my book, that war was a long time ago and we all want to forget it. I told them I am sorry we can't accommodate you eking out this so-called war hero's lecture schedule across the United States—which is all they really cared about, I bet. 'We have our own program already planned, thank you,' I told them. They just came back as cool as cats and said, 'Cancel whatever you have and fit this Varig in because he is famous.' Well, Emily, I for one never heard of him! And then they said that this Willi Varig had mentioned to their lecture series manager that he knew you, back in the 1950s, in Oslo, and National asked that you introduce him! I was so surprised! Then they said, well, he would be showing a movie about Norwegian heroes during the war and we were to provide a sixteen-millimeter movie projector. Then I saw my way out,

Emily! I told them, without mincing any words, that the projector had been lent to the Tomah, Wisconsin, Chapter of Tusend Hjem, and they hadn't returned it yet because it was broken and they wanted to get it fixed before they sent it back. Then National got sassy with me and said there were millions of people in St. Paul and Minneapolis and didn't we know anyone who would trust us with a projector? The upshot of it was, Tomah did finally send our projector back, and you were nice enough to say you *would* introduce this Varig—so we have to just hope it is all fixed up O.K. But I can tell you, Emily, without fear of its going any further, that Mrs. Thorstad was really hurt when I had to explain to her that we wouldn't want her knitting program for tonight. But anyway, I am glad it is you doing the introducing, Emily. You two were always such good Tusend Hjem members. And I guess we ought to be grateful to have this famous speaker. Apparently he is talking to all kinds of groups, not just Tusend Hjem chapters, but the American Legion and VFW posts and goodness knows what all else. So finally all I said was, O.K.—but you make sure he gets here on time and that he is sober, too! The last speaker they sent us had had a good deal to drink. Everyone noticed it. Now they promised this one would be here no later than 7:30 and it is already twenty to eight and he isn't here that I can see!" Mr. Elvekrog looked closely into Emily's eyes. "Emily, does he drink as far as you know?" he asked in a low voice.

"It is a long time since I knew Willi," Emily told him. "In 1955. But National is right about at least one thing," she went on in an encouraging tone. "He really was a very great hero in the war." She forebore to tell Mr. Elvekrog that she had never once, during the whole winter when she and her husband had known Willi, seen the hero sober or even middling-sober. It had always been the same: They would be eating cod and boiled potatoes in the smoky, workmen's restaurant above some shops in Drammensveien, while Willi and any one of his various vivid girlfriends would tell stories. Then Willi would leave them to go out into the town. He would drink his way down past Karl Johansgate until he got to the railroad station or the harbor. Much later the police brought him home, to the flat of whoever the girlfriend of the moment was. However, Willi, like Emily herself, was much older now—he might even be sixty. Perhaps he was changed.

"If that speaker doesn't show up, I won't know what to think!" cried Mr. Elvekrog.

Emily said, "If he doesn't show up, I will tell the group what he did during the war and then Mrs. Thorstad can show us the Norwegian knitting patterns if she brought them, or we can ask her questions at least."

Now it was eight o'clock. The hall had filled, and Tusend Hjem members kept turning their heads about from the seats to see if the speaker had come. Mr. Elvekrog flitted back and forth between the projector, which he wouldn't trust anyone else with, and the speaker's microphone on the podium. He pretended to check the silver-taping of the wires along the aisle. Little slips on which he had jotted the announcements kept fluttering from his fingers. Chuck Iversen, the club wit, would rescue them and make jokes to everyone. "Mr. Elvekrog? Mr. Elvekrog? Did you drop this?" he would call, waving a slip over people's heads. He pretended to be making out difficult handwriting. "It says here," he shouted, "that Mrs. Thorstad has promised to send five boxes of fattigmenn to every member of the United States Congress? Can that be right, Mrs. Thorstad?" Everyone laughed and clapped and Mrs. Thorstad grew pink and her eyes got shy as a girl's. People settled to enjoying Chuck's sideshow effects. If their speaker was some big shot too important to bother to show up at their chapter on time, then they darned well, they told each other with grins, had their own people to amuse them, and their own jokes that the speaker wouldn't understand anyway. The older members began passing around the smeary purple-dittoed copies of the Norwegian national anthem, and young people concentrated, biting their lips, some of them, trying to think up good jokes to call out, the way Chuck Iversen did.

At last, they all heard the heavy door open on the first floor. It slammed shut with a rattle of night chains. A male voice made a sharp remark; there was an equally sharp return in a higher, feminine voice, and feet started up the staircase. Definitely, then, two people were coming—very slowly considering how late they were.

It was Willi Varig. At the top of the staircase, he hung onto the handrail newel for a moment, staring round with a red, burly face. Emily recognized him despite the twenty-five years and she went lightly along a side aisle to shake hands with him. At his side stood a woman of thirty or less, who appeared to be supporting him with one arm. She reminded Emily of all of Willi's women in Oslo; it was the same startlingly pretty, rather impatient sort of girl, who would fling herself down to join them at dinner, toss off her SAS jacket and immediately regale them all with a story of what some idiot had done at Fornebu Airport or on an Air France newspaper-delivery flight.

Willi had always had a cynical cast to his nature: he liked a story told with exasperation. He would slam the girl an affectionate blow on the shoulder blade and cry, "A woman deserves a drink when she has been through what you have been through!"

Now he smiled rather unpleasantly into Emily's face and shook her hand very hard, with single jerk, in the Norwegian way. He gave a laugh. "All these years! And you have not changed a little!" he said. "I would recognize you anywhere! You do not mind if I shake your hand, I hope?" He introduced the two women, getting their names eventually. In a raucous tone, in loud English, he remarked to the Norwegian girl, "Now this is an American woman that you shake hands with! You do not dare to give her a kiss—not this one! Oh no! No, you do not do that with this one! She would explain to you that she was married already! She would not hit you across the face—she wouldn't do that! She would tell you that she admired you—Oh yes! All that wonderful admiration! But no kisses—not even for old time's sake! So we shake hands!"

The Norwegian woman brought out the bland, stewardess smile which serves a million cold situations. Emily saw Mr. Elvekrog approaching, with his desperate, creased forehead. She introduced him in Norwegian to the two vistors and told him *sotto voce* that she would introduce Willi in two minutes, not four, and that she felt he ought not to try giving the announcements before the anthem. If Willi stayed on his feet another five minutes, she thought, he would just be able to give a three-minute talk. Then he could capsize all he liked, because Mr. Elvekrog could order the lights out and start the film without him.

Supported a little by the girl, Willi began hobbling forward. The two of them tried to pass the projector in the aisle at the same time. Mr. Elvekrog's chair went over and Willi's hip gave the projector itself a smash, but Mr. Elvekrog leapt to the other side and kept it from going over onto the floor. The room was utterly silent. At the podium, waiting until Mr. Elvekrog should have settled the Norwegians in two reserved seats in the center of the first row, Emily decided she would further shorten her introduction, from the look of things—and she would not bet two cents on Willi's being able to carry off a discussion period after the film at all.

Then she smiled to the audience and said, "Good evening! I

think we will sing the anthem and have the announcements after the speaker tonight, instead of in our usual order. Before I introduce the speaker, though, I *would* like to make one very important announcement. Mrs. Thorstad *will* be showing Tusend Hjem her Norwegian knitting patterns next meeting: we will not get beat out of that!"

Emily then said it was an honor to present a speaker who was a genuine hero. "We haven't a great many real heroes," she told them. "But Willi Varig is one." She told them that Willi had belonged to a group of four Underground agents who sent information back to England from Lofthus, Hardanger, on the west coast of Norway. Willi was caught by the Germans in May of 1944. They questioned him about the names of his colleagues so that they could gather them in as well. Willi's World War II, Emily told them, was fought alone in a cellar which held two other people, both of whom were members of the enemy. They were Gestapo officers who were skilled in making people give them the information they needed. Now," Emily continued, "the only reason I have told you even this much—when I know that you want to hear the speaker himself—is that I am afraid he won't tell you that he was an extraordinarily brave man. It is an honor to present to you Willi Varig."

Emily took a seat which Mrs. Thorstad, all smiles, energetically pointed out to her, next to herself. Willi made it to the microphone. He turned a belligerent face to Emily and spoke so closely into the mike that his words racketed: "Well then!" he shouted. "I didn't know I was such a hero then! I feel as if I were attending my own funeral sermon!" He gave a rough, very loud laugh, looking about between the rims of his eyelids, expecting the audience to laugh with him. Emily was one of theirs, however, and in any case, they didn't understand his sardonic tone. Most important of all, he was visibly drunk. He looked as if his knees were about to give way.

"It is an honor to address you!" he went on, "since we fought on the same side of the war. I know that the American Legion represents the very bravest of America's veterans!"

Willi's girlfriend leaned forward as if to correct him. But then she sighed, crossed her arms, and leaned back. Mr. Elvekrog halfstood at the projector, and called in his quavering tone, "Herr Varig? This is the Minnesota Chapter of Tusend Hjem!"

Willi pounded his fist on the podium, as if to make a salient point, and then said, only, in a kind of snarl: "I think we will now have the film, please, if you will close the lights."

In the sudden, grateful darkness, the people could hear their speaker stumbling back towards his seat. The screen lighted up.

"Norsk Film A/S," the screen told them in white print on black. Then white, typed credits appeared in jerks over clips of a young woman tapping wireless messages under the speckled shade of camouflage; three figures sneaked up under a bridge on which a German-helmeted soldier was slowly walking, occasionally glancing overside; two Norwegian girls smiled widely at two Gestapo officers leaving a wooden hut. But the instant the door was shut, one girl crouched at it, listening, while the other quickly lifted a *dynetrekk* and folded it back, revealing a radio set. She put on a pair of earphones and immediately began sending.

Then, all of a sudden, the projector clattered. Mr. Elvekrog gave an exclamation, the screen whitened with lightning and tortured patterns, the aisle area began to reek of burnt celluloid. In the next instant, Mr. Elvekrog called sharply, "Someone turn the lights on please!" Other, younger, more resonant men's voices added, "Yes—someone get the lights back there!"

People rubbed their eyes in the brightness. They turned to Mr. Elvekrog, who sat beside the projector with curls and curls of movie-tape bunched and falling about his lap and legs. With his bleak expression, he looked like a provincial actor who has just removed an elaborate Louis XVI wig.

Chuck Iversen cried out, "Well, I see that the Tomah Chapter didn't repair the projector too good! So much for lending things to the neighbors is what I say!"

People tittered. They were not a club that relished documentaries anyway. They had been resigned to the film, because they knew that at least coffee and krullers would follow sooner or later. Now it would be sooner, they saw, and they cheered up. With the projector broken, and the fellows beginning to act up, there might be some fun.

Here and there, men stood up and put their hands into their pockets. They wandered back to the cleared area behind all the auditorium seating, away from the women and the others who passively waited in their seats. Meanwhile, Mr. Elvekrog bent over the film feeder. The teeth had somehow shredded some film edge and left celluloid about like auger tailings on the floor. He said in anguish to Emily, who had come back to see if she could help: "National is going to raise a fuss about this! I just know they are!"

Minutes passed. At last, Chuck Iversen shouted to everyone generally, "So what is wrong with singing *Ja, vi elsker dette landet* and having the coffee and cookies? History lessons or cookies, give me cookies every time!"

Someone in the rear, from the knot of men who were changing their weight from foot to foot, shouted, "You don't have any culture, Chuck, is what your trouble is!"

Chuck shouted back, when people stopped laughing: "Oh, to get my hands on the fellow that got off *that* remark!"

The moment was passing into the hands of the people.

"Willi has completely passed out," Emily whispered to Mr. Elvekrog, bending over him while handling film as if she were helping him with the mechanics of repair. "Do you want me to go up and explain very fast exactly what he did during the war and then announce the anthem and you can do the announcements and we will have the lunch?"

"Oh, would you?" cried the program committee chairman.

Up at the podium, Emily waited for silence, glancing over at the Norwegian speaker. He lay oddly twisted on the woman's lap, his left hand hung down between the thighs of her expensive trousers, his face buried in her stomach as her hand patted his shoulder.

Emily said into the p.a. system, "If we can all somehow get Chuck Iversen to shut up for a second!"

This brought her the laugh she needed.

Then she went on, fast: "Here is what we will do. I am going to tell you very briefly what Willi Varig did. I will keep it down to a few minutes—and then we will do the anthem and announcements and have our coffee. Is that O.K. with all of you?"

There were nods, almost everywhere in the room, and the scattered muttering directed not to one another in the rows but directly from individual people to her, which Emily knew meant the people were relieved—a leader is taking over and it will all get solved.

Emily told the group about the German invasion of Norway, in April, 1940. She told them how the Norwegian Underground kept in touch with the RAF and British Intelligence through air drops, radio, telegraph—and when things were very wrong, through escape via small boats across the North Sea.

"When I first knew Willi Varig, however," Emily said, "it was ten years after the war. My husband and I lived in Oslo on a Fulbright—and German tourists were just beginning to come into Norway again. Willi used to be drunk nearly every night. We would have dinner with him, in a small students' dining room in Drammensveien, which I am sure many of you have walked in during your summer visits to Norway. Then, after dinner, Willi would wander down to the Ostbanestasjonen by himself." Emily paused to let the Norwegian-Americans proudly whisper back and forth to one another, "Ostbanestasjonen—the East railway station!"

"Willi would wander along close behind the groups of tourists getting off the train, deliberately listening to their talk of getting porters, finding hotels, and so on. He paid no attention to the younger ones with their rucksacks and knee-socks. They weren't what he wanted. He followed those of about thirty or more. When he had determined they were Germans he would catch up with whichever man appeared to be the father or the leader and say, in his perfect schoolboy German, 'I beg your pardon, sir, but is the Herr visiting Norway for the first time?' The polite German would get over his surprise at being addressed by a stranger. In the next moment, he would be charmed by this Norwegian in his good shirt and tie and sports jacket—and sometimes Willi even went down to the train in his dinner coat—and the German would smile and say, 'Well—no, actually, it *isn't* my first time! I have seen Norway before! And I told myself then, that when I married, the first thing I would do is bring my wife back to this so beautiful country and I would show her the wonderful mountains! I especially think the Hardanger plateau is beautiful! But of course, your city, Oslo, is beautiful as well!' Then, Willi, smiling, would say, 'Ah, then, the Herr was in Norway a long time ago and is returning with pleasure? I can understand that!' and the German, poor sap, would respond, 'Not a *long* time ago—I was stationed here during the War in fact—and grew very much to love this country!' That, of course, is what Willi was waiting for, so then he would put a heavy hand to the German's shoulder, bringing him to a stop. They had been walking along, with the baggage man and his cart ahead of them. When Willi stopped the German, the baggage man stopped at the same moment, before even looking around. Still smiling now, Willi would say, 'And would the Herr have any idea that when people love a thing—a person or their own country—they do not like to have it taken away?' and before the German could see the turn the conversation had taken, Willi would have struck him as hard as he could manage in the man's face. The German generally fell down, unless Willi was so drunk he missed his mark. People stood around waiting for the man to rise. Norwegian railway officials went through the motions of linking their arms around Willi's elbows. The baggage man turned forward again and pulled the cart as if nothing had happened. Soon you would hear the Oslo two-toned police sound. Everyone made a little way for the police. 'Right, Willi!' they said briskly, 'In you go!' and they popped him into their car. Dozens of people knew the routine perfectly well. Back at the station, the policemen would give Willi some coffee and drive him sedately back up Karl Johansgate, past the castle, up Drammensveien, and deliver him to his woman of the moment."

Emily went on, "That was eleven years after Willi's war was over. He had been laying a flare path near Stavali, on the Hardanger plateau, in preparation for an RAF equipment drop. He was caught by the Germans. Willi noticed, with satisfaction, that, when the patrol arrested him, his friends, who were two men and a woman, had vanished. That meant they knew that he had been taken and that they had not been seen: that was important. Once anyone was taken prisoner, the others had to use the pre-planned flight to the sea. Anyone captured would talk, sooner or later, so you simply had to run either east to Sweden or west and south to England. Willi's group kept a shabby fishing boat at Lofthus, with its dinghy shoved under what looked like an abandoned dock. It was arranged that a fisherman take their sailboat out nearly every other day, letting himself be seen on deck, making small repairs, running her sail up and down, trying different engine richnesses. The German coast patrols had trained their glasses on the man for so long they knew his figure by heart—the thick white sweater he wore even on the hottest days when he must have sweltered, and even on the coldest days when he would have been better off with a stormcoat like the other fishermen.

"The Germans took Willi to the nearest office," Emily explained. "A pleasant-spoken young Gestapo officer told Willi that all they really needed were the names of his immediate colleagues and a few practical details. These details would be useful to them, the man explained, with a rueful tone, who had to go on fighting the tiresome war, but not to Willi since he would be able to relax now, in prison. They needed to know his radio frequencies, and the summer's drop plans. At least for now, they told him, that was all they needed. Willi felt he had an hour before he would be made to talk. The German officer would be willing to spend an hour in establishing a trust relationship; beyond that, he would know that Willi was stalling. But up to an hour, he might feel that Willi saw reason and would tell him what he needed for his report. An hour would take Willi's friends from the flare site to Stavali, and another two hours would get them down the steep mountainside to Lofthus. The hour passed as if it were two minutes. The German went out a moment and brought back in with him a colleague whom he politely introduced by name. The colleague knelt by Willi's chair and proceeded to loosen Willi's right kneecap with a screw. Then the colleague, or someone, splashed water on Willi, and when he came to they began again. The second time he came to, he found only the original officer in the room with him. 'You know, Willi, if I may call you by your first name? In a few years' time, perhaps in only one year, the war will be over, and I will go back to Germany and be married and raise a family. I would like my son to go to Berlin—the University. And the same for you, Willi. You will return to your Oslo and marry and have a family—you will watch your children waving flags on May 17th with all the other children— and later, you will watch them strolling around in their student caps. And we will both get old, but gradually, easily—in the leisure of time, Willi! You in your beautiful country, Willi, and I in mine! And there is not a soul on earth who will remember what was said or done, in this room, today. What is a single spring day in 1944 when it has gotten to be 1970, 1980, or perhaps even 1990?' He paused. 'If you tell me what I have to know simply because it is my job, I will arrange for you to live, Willi. If you make us *make* you tell us, you will probably die—but in any case, we would shoot you. And you know better than to think you won't talk! Everyone talks! How is your knee now? You know, Willi, when my colleague comes in again, he will not stick only to the right knee. Next time it will be the other knee. I can check on it—but I am pretty sure that is how they do it. They pretty much follow the same routine each time ... first the one, then the other. Then after the war I will go back to Germany and marry and raise my family—and my wife will never know that I spent today making a prisoner talk in this room. And of course you will be dead, so you will never have a wife.' Here the intelligence officer paused, and then he added, making the only mistake he had made: 'Willi, everyone talks! . . . *sooner or later.*' "

Emily paused herself and then went on. "The German's mistake was in saying 'sooner or later.' This reminded Willi that talking sooner was not at all the same as talking several hours later. What he had to do was wipe out of his mind's eye the picture of 1970, 1980, 1990, which the German had kept painting for him—the picture of the gentle future when all would be peaceful and wonderful for those still alive to enjoy it. He needed to put some other picture into his mind's eye—and keep it there—for one hour, for two hours if he could. He needed to imagine his friends, the two Underground men and the woman, who would, if Willi did not talk right away, scramble down the rocky path behind Lofthus, shove the dinghy out from under its rotten boarding, and row out to the fishingboat which always stood at its mooring. He had to force this image into his mind, over and over—and what helped him to do it was the German's saying 'sooner or later.' So now he said to himself, 'If I last ten minutes more, they have reached the dock. I wonder if dark is coming on now—but I mustn't trust to that, because it is getting on for Sankthansaften and the days are extraordinarily long. If I last,' Willi thought—for now the second German had returned to the cellar room and was kneeling at the other side of Willi's chair, 'if I last another ten minutes, they are all in the dinghy now and they are saying, "Good old Willi! He must not have talked yet!" Now I think I will not last a whole another ten minutes but I could do five, I think, because the fjord is quiet and the motor started right up without any trouble. And now my friend has put on that filthy white sweater which was left right where it was supposed to be and he has the tiller and the others hidden below are sending on the wireless; they are already asking for help now! Thank God then, the motor started up all right for them! And now the Germans are looking at the boat quietly going out the main fjord and saying, "Oh—there's that idiot in the white sweater and that wreck of a boat again!" Then Willi told himself, 'I do not remember my friends' names anyway. I do not know how many there were of them. I do not remember them. There may have been five, there may have been six. And soon they will be out to sea, and the man in the white sweater will be joined by the people who now can come topside out of hiding. They have sent their wireless call for help, and someone in England or on the Sea and in the

Channel has heard, and someone in turn rang up Air/Sea Rescue and they had better have got her mainsail up now—in just this last minute I think they did get their mainsail up all right!' Then when he had passed out again and the enemy had brought him to again, Willi said to himself, 'I should say they have picked up a several-force wind out there, but it is from the North so they are running southward to England, south by west, and there is not much difficulty with the waves because they are running with them, but it is rough and the sea is chopped up by the wind.' When Willi woke up the next time he saw in his mind's eye that at last it was night. A submarine rose, shedding a white robing of sea from its bilges, and even after her captain appeared at the conning tower, water slid gently and uniformly off her deck and bilges. The captain was a young Englishman and he shouted at the crew of a Norwegian fishing vessel. The Norwegians brought their boat about so she shuddered now into the wind, and the Englishmen sent over two sailors in a rubber boat. At the submarine, the Norwegian woman handed up a canvas bag and said, 'Will you be so kind as to sink our boat, please, as she may give away information?' The Englishman and his guncrew and the Norwegians watched, their jaws shaking with cold, as the bullets struck the little fishing boat at the waterline. Then the English captain cried, 'Right! Now! Down below with all of you!' The three Underground agents went gingerly below, their feet now gone so cold they felt nothing at the knees and below. They sank gingerly down the rungs and into the oddly motherly, smelly warmth of the sub. Then Willi made the picture in his mind of the submarine's smooth round side frothing and slipping below the huge waves of the North Sea. It moved with its electric ease, far under the tortured waves.

"Then Willi talked. He told the Gestapo officer the names of the two men and the woman. But you see," Emily said heavily to the Tusend Hjem members, "he talked later, not sooner. His partners did make it to England. Then, Germans being Germans, they repaired Willi's knees fairly well. As you all noticed tonight, Willi doesn't walk perfectly, but he does walk.

"And now I am done talking," Emily told them, "but for one thing. If you will please all look over to where Willi is now."

Those sitting near Willi and his girlfriend had already been peeping, anyhow. The girl, with Willi's hand still dangling between her legs, glared at no one in particular with her composed, inimical expression. People towards the rear stood up and peered over heads. People whispered. "Now what I am asking of Tusend Hjem is," Emily said, "that we choose. We can keep a kind of mental picture of this Willi here, the one you are looking at right now—or, you can imagine him in your mind's eye, strapped in a chair, with the German intelligence officers. The one who spoke so pleasantly, and the one with the screws. You can remember that scene."

Then Mr. Elvekrog came forward, wiping something from the projector off his hands. He gave the announcements, he led them in the Norwegian anthem. Presently, Emily was able to drive the twenty minutes home to White Bear Lake. Mist still rose, more strongly than before, from all the hollows alongside I-35 E. She felt peaceful and absent-minded, and hoped that her daughter would be in bed and the house would be dark and still.

She brought the car very slowly into the drive, so as not to wake Sandra in case she were asleep. Then she crept out and decided to have a look over the lake in the dark. But impressions from the house would creep in, and disturb her mood. She could not help thinking how unhappy her daughter was—how something either major or minor was wrong with Sandra's marriage. She felt, with what she hoped was mistaken intuition, that her daughter was interested in someone other than her husband.

The mist over White Bear Lake was absolutely solid now. The water itself was invisible in the mist and the night, but she felt its presence, so full and rich with rainwater it was nearly rounded upward.

She thought, again, of the Norwegian Underground agents. Neither she nor Willi nor anyone else would ever have the slightest notion what the three people whom Willi had saved had done with their lives. There was nothing to guarantee they had not wasted them. They may never have done anything lovely at all. Emily tried to picture the woman of that Underground team. If she were still alive, she would be old by now. Perhaps she had married for love— but perhaps she had then met someone else, later, who stirred her somehow as she had never imagined possible, but perhaps she did not marry this other person, but stayed with the husband. But then, Emily thought, so many years have passed—likely one or both of the men are dead now. Or perhaps they are utterly dull.

Still, Emily felt herself growing elated, as she stood there staring out over the fog. She did not really have in her mind's eye a picture of aged, paunchy, or lonely old Norwegians. What she really had in mind was the little sailing boat in the North Sea, with its crew young and beautiful; the sea had misted crystal into their hand-knitted caps and sweaters; their hands had chilled on the sheets and stays and tiller; their knees ably took the sea's heave—and all the time, the three of them kept looking and looking, hoping and half-knowing a powerful friend would emerge from the deep, and come up alongside, and save them.

Gunnar's Sword

A S SHE CLIMBED THE HILL to the Home, Harriet White felt the town falling away behind her. She usually despised the town in a casual, peaceful way, the way adults sometimes despise their parents' world once they've left it. The mind simply remembers it as something unpleasant, but dead. Right now she felt annoyed with the town in general because she had begun a quarrel with the Golden Age Auxiliary women about the quilts they were making: they were using old chenille bedspreads for centers, since the center can never be seen, and then doing elegant patchwork covers. The pastor had held the quilts up at service and praised the ladies. These quilts, which looked cosy but didn't keep out the cold, were then sent to the Lutheran World Relief. Harriet was irritated by these women's ethics, which were like a mix of local pastors' remarks and the inchoate philosophies of their husbands in the VFW Lounge.

She had lived all her adult life with her husband and son on their quarter section, where a half mile in every direction was theirs: when she came to the Home, she had somehow to shrink it all to the size of her room. Some people managed that by stuffing all the furniture they could bring from their old houses into the tiny rooms of the Lutheran Home; Harriet managed it by working away at her pastimes with a fury. The crafts room was full of her output; she was like a factory: she turned out more sweaters and afghans than twenty residents together. But when it snowed, even during the tiresome snows of late March, she felt a settling inside her, as if her mind lowered and glided outward, like the surface of a lake. She would fetch her coat and overshoes and walk about the ordinary, dreamless town. She felt lost in thought like someone who has been dealt with cordially.

Harriet's neck was ropy and knotted, in the way of old people

who have got thin. She forgave herself that. As a little girl, and
later as a young woman, she had feared the degradation that age
might bring. She remembered watching the hired girl, who had
cared for her over weekends when her parents went to their club,
pulling on her stockings. Above the knee, Harriet had seen the
white meat of the thigh swelling and she had sworn, I shall never
let my legs look like that! And later she had sworn, I shall never let
my chin sag like that! Or, I shall never lower myself to *that*! Now,
as she swung fairly easily up the hill, she thought she was less dis-
contented with her body, and self, than she had been at any time
earlier. She was eighty-two, but she kept a jaunty air, some of
which was gratitude when her right ankle didn't act up. She
climbed firmly, noting how soundless the cold air was, except for
traffic in the town below. The elm treetops were broomy and
vague; the smoke from the Home power plant piped slowly
straight up. She hoped it would snow.

On the upper sidewalk at last, she saw Arne, the Home's driver
and man of all work, helping Mr. Solstad, the mortician, wheel a
casket out of the east entrance. Harriet paused, partly for the flag
that lay over the coffin, and she knew it was the body of Mr. Ole
Morstad whose funeral was to be down at the church that afternoon. She was not sorry that he was dead; he had been taken up to
the infirmary floor on third more than three years ago. Then, rather
than now, they had recognized his death; her roommate, LaVonne
Morstad, had cried and Harriet had held her shoulder and hand.
"He will never come back down onto second!" cried Vonnie then.
And so he hadn't.

Arne and Mr. Solstad eased the casket off its wheeled cart into the
hearse. Then Arne came over to Harriet, with his workingman's
sidewise walk, blowing on his hands. He smiled at her. "Morning,
missus," he said respectfully, as he always did. Residents who were
very feeble or not very alert he tended to call by their Christian
names. "Will you be wanting a ride down to the services this afternoon, Mrs. White?"

"I'll walk, Arne—it isn't so cold!"

"Not for you maybe," he said admiringly. "But some of 'em,
they wouldn't go if they had to walk."

"I bet you won't be taking down storm windows today after all,"
Harriet said, remembering an announcement over the public-
address system that morning.

"Feels like snow," he said, swinging his head northwest, where the tiny cars ran along on the cold gray highway. "Weather don't seem to scare you none though."

They both paused as the hearse drove by them carefully—and then they gave each other that farm-people's signal, as they parted. It was a slight wave with the right hand—half like a staff officer's from his jeep; half like a pastor's benediction. Harriet went in.

She avoided the reception entrance, with the residents sitting about looking hot and faint, and the few children inevitably hanging around the TV sets instead of going up to the grandparents they'd been sent to visit. She marched straight off to the back, where the crafts room was, and had the good luck to find Marge Larson, the therapist, there. The room was full of half-finished products at this end—but at the other end, screened off by a Sears Roebuck room divider, was the "shop" where the finished hot pads, napkin holders, aprons were on sale. The Golden Age Auxiliary members came by regularly and bought. Harriet's work was known because it was fair isle knitting, in western Minnesota called Norwegian knitting. Not everyone could do it. Harriet also helped Marge with other people's unfinished work, or work that needed to be taken out and remade, which she kept quiet about.

Together they discussed some of the projects lying around on tables. Some weren't any good. An old man was in the room, too, but it was Orrin Bjorning who could not hear and could not work. He sat utterly still, and the dull light came in off the snow so that the skin on his forehead and cheeks looked like a hood—as if a monk sat there frozen—instead of like a face. He insisted on spending whole mornings in the crafts room, his fingers bent around a piece of 1 x 1. He never stirred. When the PA system announced dinner time, he would shake himself and slowly leave, never speaking.

Harriet and Marge walked around the room, touching and lifting Orlon, felt, acrylic, cotton. Harriet promised to return in the afternoon, and work a little on Mrs. Steensen's rug. Mrs. Steensen had started braiding. Marge often placed new lots of nicely stripped wool in the woman's lap and Mrs. Steensen always looked up and said energetically, "Yes—good, thanks then, Marge!" in her Scandinavian accent. "*Ja*—I've been needing just such a blue—now I can get on with my rug!" And then all morning, her hands made little plucking gestures at the rags in her lap. Marge and Harriet together worked up two or three feet of the braid from time to time and Mrs. Steensen seemed not to notice. "Rug's coming along pretty good!" she would shout, when Marge came by.

At ten Harriet left. She still had her coat to hang up, and she had to write a short speech. Later she would have to help Vonnie Morstad dress for the funeral.

But she stopped at the second floor landing because Mr. Helmstetter and Kermit Steensen were sitting by the elevators.

"Thank you very much for that little rabbit favor, missus," Helmstetter said. "I gave it to my granddaughter—the one they called Kristi. Kristi is for Christine, that's her aunt on the other side, then Ann for the middle name. I suppose it's for someone. She was very pleased."

"*Ja*, I suppose you told her you made it, huh," Kermit said, one of the Home wits.

Helmstetter blushed. "She wouldn't have believed that, I guess. Where you going in such a rush?" he said to Harriet. "You're always rushing. Chasing. This way, that way. Such a busy lady."

"Busier'n Jacqueline Kennedy," Kermit said.

Harriet sat down beside them and they all faced the aluminum elevator door. "I can sit down a moment."

"Work'll keep," Helmstetter said.

"Work don't run away," Kermit Steensen said in a witty tone. Again they all laughed, all of them more heartily than they felt like, but they all felt pretty cheerful for a second. Harriet rose to the occasion.

"Well, how's 'Edge of Night' coming?" Harriet asked them. She knew that they all listened to television drama serials during afternoon coffee in the coffee room. In the morning the sun didn't come into the coffee room, so it was empty save for the candystripers' carts and a slight odor of dentures. In the afternoon, however, the lace curtains were transformed and a light fell on the people as they were served their "lunch"—the western Minnesota word for the midafternoon snack. Sometimes the sun was so gorgeous that they had to squint to make out the dove-pale images on the TV set. Helmstetter and Steensen and a couple of other men—and nearly all the second floor women—kept track of the dramas. From time to time, Harriet asked them about the plots.

"We don't watch that anymore," Kermit told her. "'Splendor of Our Days' is what we're watching now."

"This young fellow has got an incurable disease and he is trying not to tell his girl about it, but she knows. She wants to talk it over with him so she can help him."

"Oh, that isn't the point!" Kermit said sharply. "The point is he doesn't want her to find out he's scared to die. He wants to keep on laughing and joking right up to the end. She belongs to the country club that his folks want to get into."

"There's an old Viking story like that," Harriet put in. "Do you remember that old legend about how the Vikings believed you must make a joke before you died, in order to show Death you were better than he is?"

Letting the *Lutheran Herald* sag on his knees, Helmstetter said courteously, "How'd that hang together then?"

Harriet said, "There was a particular young Viking and he and his friends had a grudge against a man named Gunnar. So one day they decided they would put a ladder up to the loft where Gunnar slept, while he was away, then they'd hide in there and then kill him when he came in at night. So the friends helped the young fellow put up the ladder, and up he went, with his knife between his teeth. Just as he was heaving himself over the windowsill, however, Gunnar, who happened not to be away after all, leapt off his straw bed and ran his sword right through the young Viking. The Viking fell off the ladder backward. His friends raced over to where he lay, with the blood coursing out of his chest.

"'Oh—Gunnar is at home, then?' they asked with astonishment.

"'Well now,' the young man said as he died, 'I don't know if Gunnar is home but his sword is.'"

Helmstetter and Steensen hesitated: they weren't sure they got the point of the story, yet they felt moved. "Pretty good, pretty good," they both murmured. There was a polite pause, and then Kermit Steensen fidgeted and brightened and said, "Not to change the subject, you see this girl belongs to the country club, but the boyfriend isn't interested at all, but all the time his parents are anxious for him to belong and they keep throwing him together with this girl."

"But she's really interested in that other fellow—the doctor fellow!" cried Helmstetter with a laugh.

"She isn't either!" said Steensen. "That was all over weeks ago. In fact they've dropped him; you don't see him anymore."

"I seen him on there just yesterday!"

"You see lots of things!" Helmstetter said.

Harriet rose after a moment, and said, "Are you going to be in the dining room at 11?''

"What for then?" Both old men were very anxious not to be for-
getful of any part of the Home schedule.

"We're having coffee in honor of Marge Larson, you know, the
woman who helps us with crafts? It's her birthday. We'd do it this
afternoon but there's the Morstad funeral."

"Oh, *ja*, then," the men said. When Harriet left, they fingered
the church magazines on their knees in a distracted sort of way, and
Kermit began deliberately snapping over the pages.

Harriet looked forward to getting to her room. She not only had
two books going at the same time but she also had one small bit of
knitting—a patterned complicated sweater for little Christopher.
She had not used a pattern, but had counted the stitches there were
to be across the shoulders, at front and back, and then, using the
same number of squares on light-blue-inked graph paper, she had
made up her own pattern. She blocked in the colors with crayons,
trying different combinations. It was immensely satisfying, because she not only had the problem of what colors and shapes would
look well in wool, but also, she wanted, if possible, to make up a
pattern that would work in the different colors in any one row at
least as often as every fifth stitch. If a row were to have blue and white,
for example, she made sure the blue yarn was used at least as often
as once in five—or the white, conversely. This way she prevented
"carrying" yarn for more than an inch in the back. Long, carried
yarn tended to get caught in buttons and baby fingers. Harriet
laughed at herself for her love of knitting—you are simple-
minded, she told herself—yet it sustained her in a way that would
have surprised her years before. For example, during the meals—as
in most institutions meals were a weak side of life at the Home—
she could keep cheerful and even hold up a sort of one-handed conversation, by reminding herself that the orderly, beautiful knitting
lay waiting upstairs. Sometimes the thought of her knitting even
came to her during Larry's visits. I do hope, she told herself, I
won't get so my own son is overshadowed by a pair of worsted mit-
tens. She felt certain that the best defense of one's personality,
against everything—senility mostly, and worse, later—was one's
humor. And hers was intact. Or at least, so people assured her.

"You have a wonderful sense of humor, Mother," Larry had told
her on one of his visits from Edina. "When did you develop it? Was
it when you married Dad and went into farming?"

She opened her top bureau drawer to take out the lined paper
to write the speech for Marge on, and found Larry's last letter. "I'm
hoping to get out to Jacob over the weekend, hopefully Saturday,"
he wrote. Ghastly usage, Harriet thought affectionately. "I'll call
Saturday around noon if I do. Are you having a cold horrible
March? The city is a mess — mud and melting snow. I don't know
why we Minnesotans complain about winter, spring is what's horrible. See you soon. Love from us all, a kiss from that wonderful
little Christopher — Larry." Harriet read it over again, and then
laid it under her notebook.

She began work on the speech. "We are gathered here this morning in honor of Marge's birthday," she began. "But it seems to me
it would make a lot more sense if she were gathered here in honor
of *our* birthdays — we've had so many more of them." She sat back,
staring at the smudgy storm window that Arne had not removed.
"What drivel," she thought, glancing at her speech again. She
crossed it out. Even first-rate jokes didn't work particularly well at
the Home — and second-rate jokes went very badly. She visualized
the dining room — the bleached foreheads, held motionless over the
plates full of desserts, the stately, plastic flowers. She bent to the
job again, forcing herself not to hope that Larry might offer her a
ride out into the country to look at the farm. She worked away at
the speech, finished, shortened it, and had just thought to check the
time when Vonnie came in.

The young girl volunteers called candy-stripers had put curlers
in Vonnie's hair for her. On the first floor was a shampooing room,
where once a week a few members of the Jacob Lutheran
Church — the Golden Age Auxiliary — laid their heavy coats on the
steel-tubing chairs, and washed and set the hair of any of the
women who cared to come down. In between those Tuesday afternoons, the candy-stripers would sometimes do it. The residents
preferred the services of the Golden Age women, most of whom
were in their fifties and could remember how hair "should be done
nice" — meaning, with bobby pins screwed to the head, dried hard,
and then brushed and combed, leaving discernible curls. The
young girls, on the other hand, believed in either back-combed
hair — or more recently, in simply straight "undone" hair. Vonnie
came into the room scowling, and Harriet supposed she wasn't
pleased with the way the candy-stripers had done her.

"Shall we lay out our clothes for this afternoon?" Harriet said,
closing her notebook.

Vonnie grasped the arms of her rocking chair, got ready, and then jammed herself down into it. "You lay out *your* clothes!"

"Can I help?" Harriet said gently.

"I can lay out my own clothes; I can get into my own clothes. Next thing you'll want to rinse my teeth!"

"Going to the dining room for the birthday coffee for Marge?" Harriet said after a pause.

"To hear your speech you mean!" snapped Vonnie. Her cheeks shook.

"Vonnie!"

"Oh, *ja*, Vonnie! Don't Vonnie me!" cried the woman. "I am sick of you doing everything like you were better than everyone else. Speech for Marge! Why couldn't we of got a printed card like everyone wanted? A nice printed card, with a nice picture, a photo of some roses, on nice paper with a nice poem on it, they got hundreds now, at either one of the drugstores—you're always going on them walks, you could of walked to the drugstore and you could have got it and you could of read it aloud to us, and then we would have the cake and it would be real nice. But oh no, you got to do some fancy thing no one ever thought of—oh, *ja*, it had to be something—a speech!"

"Ridiculous," Harriet said. "A woman like Marge gets a hundred cards like that a year. The idea is to do something more personal."

"Whose idea? Everyone else thought a card would be real nice!"

Vonnie turned around and faced Harriet—the day's full light on her stretched forehead. "And I got something else to say to you also! My knitting! You can just keep to your own and leave my work alone! When I want your help with my work, I'll ask you for it."

"Oh, Vonnie," Harriet said, "all we did was take out back to the row where the increasing was supposed to start, and do the increasing every second row—and then you take over again from there."

"Don't you have any of your own to do? Why don't you do your own increasing and your own decreasing and leave mine be."

They both stood up and stiffly began taking fresh stockings, their better shoes, their dark print dresses out of their closets. If they dressed now, they wouldn't be caught dressing later when LaVonne's relations began coming in to pick her up to go down to the church. They had a half hour before the birthday coffee for Marge.

When they both were dressed, there was a pause. There was a problem they simply had to solve: Vonnie's hair. Harriet finally took the lead. "Vonnie," she said as efficiently and impersonally as she could, "let's get your curlers out now—because now's when we've got time to get it combed out before LeRoy and Mervin come."

The widow grumbled, but let herself down in her chair, with her eyes pointed coldly into the mirror. "I don't want it brushed out too much. I don't like the way that one candy-striper girl does it. No sense of how hair should be done."

"The one called Mary?" Harriet asked. Standing behind Vonnie, she began gently taking out curlers.

"*Ja.* Now that other one's a real nice girl. Friend of the Helmstetters. My Mervin married a Helmstetter." Slowly the curlers came off—LaVonne Morstad kept one trembling wrist raised, to receive them one by one from Harriet. Talking to each other in the mirror, the two women pulled together again, a little.

The chaplain's voice now came over the PA system: his voice was rusty and idealistic. In his Scandinavian accent, he said: "If everyone will please come straight down to the dining room, we will be having a coffee hour in honor of Mrs. Marge Larson. If everyone will please come down to the dining room, we will be having a coffee hour in honor of Mrs. Marge Larson. *Vil De vaer så snill å komme til spisesalen; vi skal ha kaffe . . .*" continuing in Norwegian. He did not give his announcement in German, for in the Jacob area most of the German-Americans were Catholics. There were only a dozen or so in the Lutheran Home.

Harriet left Vonnie muttering over the funeral programs. The widow had the conviction something had been printed incorrectly, and she kept running her big finger across the lines again, pronouncing the names, the thou's and thee's, in a hoarse whisper.

Harriet found Marge and Arne dragging the PA system hookup over to the standing mike, near the diabetic table. Now the younger residents came in briskly, glancing out at the snow-lit window, nodding to one another. The more aged people followed, looking like the wooden carvings of Settesdal valley and the Jotenheim. Over the shuffling slippers, the stooped backs were immobile; you were aware of the folds and creases of sleeves, the velvety skin coating elbows that looked sore, the huge blocky ankles of the old, like knots of marble. Harriet listened, a little nervous as always before she addressed a group, aware of rayon rubbing, now chair legs being dragged out. Finally everyone was seated—even old Orrin Bjorning sat gazing at his right hand cupped over his left. Harriet was delighted to find Kermit Steensen and some of the other men sitting where she could see them; if you had just a face or two responding, you could carry the others.

"Harriet," Marge said, "would you read off the birthday list for this month? We were going to do it for Golden Age this afternoon, but since most of them will be down at the funeral, we thought we'd better do it this morning."

Harriet flattened the typed yellow sheet over her clipboard, rapidly checking the names for those she might not pronounce right. Three were crossed through—she recognized the names of two men who had died in the past few weeks, and of a woman whose relatives had moved her to the Dawson Nursing Home. Mr. Ole Morstad's name was still on. "Shan't I pencil through this?" Harriet asked, pointing.

"Oh my goodness—thanks!" cried Marge, leaning across Harriet to run her ball-point through it. "I'm glad you caught that!"

They stood together, planning the next few minutes—odd, Harriet thought, this stupid 15-minute affair, a two-minute speech for a birthday, and yet it had all the trappings of the hundreds of meetings she had presided over. It had also the old lilt to it—the sense that she herself was exciting, someone who could bring off things, someone to be relied on; if little difficulties arose, she could back and fill. She was a leader. Color came up into her face and she knew it.

As Arne knelt at her feet tinkering with the extension cord, Harriet thought, I used to believe that as I got old I'd feel closer to people of all sorts of backgrounds. I thought there was some great common denominator we'd all sink to—and I'd feel *more* affectionate toward clumsy, or inexperienced people. But it hasn't worked out. I don't! I am perfectly resigned to being among people who never read or reflect on anything but I don't feel close. And less than ever can I understand how they can bear life with one another. She looked out, now, over the whole dining room because Arne was through, and her birthday list, touching the mike, gave a hoarse rattle, showing the current was on.

"Good morning!" she said, remembering not to duck to the mike. "We are gathered together this morning in honor of someone who means a great deal to every one of us." She went on, faces turned toward her. Quietly, at the edges of the room, the kitchen staff with their red wrists carried in coffee urns and set down plates of dessert. Harriet noticed with the speed of eight years' residency that the dessert was sawed slices of angel food with Wilderness Cherry Pie filling and Cool Whip on it. She was aware of Marge herself, modestly perched on a chair at the diabetic table. When the speech was over, and the gift received, Marge would be off again—flying around doing the dozens of chores she somehow accomplished during a day—pushing a wheelchair to the shampoo room, helping a church women's group plan their surprises for the infirmary trays, even helping to tip the vats of skinned potatoes in the kitchen. Harriet mentioned some of these tasks so graciously done—and she heard the warmth fill in her voice. It had its effect, too. She had the people's attention: the moment she saw that, she felt still another warmth in her voice: the warmth of success. So she wound up with some lilt, made Marge stand, handed over the gift, excused the roomful of people from singing "Happy Birthday" because she knew they hated it—the sound of their awful voices—and she read the birthday list, after which everyone clapped. Then she said to Marge, "We all say, bless you, Marge," and retreated from the microphone.

Harriet settled herself in a folding chair by the maids' serving stand to hear Marge's thanks, but Siegert, the head nurse, was bending over her shoulder: "It's your son, Mrs. White. He's waiting for you in your room. I said you'd come up, but surely you can stay and have your coffee . . ."

"No, no!" cried Harriet. "I'm coming! Larry! No, I don't want any coffee! Thanks, Mrs. Siegert!"

The nurse smiled. "Tell you what, I'll bring up some of the dessert for both of you—and some coffee, how's that?"

˙ "How nice you are," Harriet cried, and hurried out.

She wanted to go the fastest way, which is to say, up the staircase, but then she would be short of breath when she arrived and then Larry would worry. So she pressed the stupid bell and waited for the poky elavator to sink all the way down from the infirmary on third.

She found room 211 full of Morstad men. They were milling about in the tiny space between the bureaus, the two rocking chairs, the beds—in heavy dark overcoats flung open in the hot air of the Home. They were shaking hands, in turns, and then prowling about the room, trying not to bump into one another or the

radiator. Vonnie herself stood rummaging in the top drawer of her
bureau. Her rocking chair kept rocking as one man or another
struck it with his ankes. Harriet paused a moment, daunted by the
crowd, and then entered, and shook hands with each person sepa-
rately. They were in their good clothes. "I think I ought to know
yer face . . . Mervin Morstad's my name. My brother LeRoy, Mrs.
White. He's from the Cities—over in Edina. Well I guess you know
our mother all right." (Sociable laughter.) ". . . Deepest sympathy."
"Oh, thank you now. . . . Yes, he was. He sure was—a blessing in a
way, if you get how I mean. . . . Here—mother, never mind—it
don't matter. . . ."

But Vonnie was furious. "Don't matter! I'll say it does. Look,
right there, in print, and we paid for it, too!"

Both her sons, Mervin and LeRoy, huge men with gleaming,
round cheeks, tipped their gigantic shoulders like circling air-
planes over the card she held. She handed it to Mervin, and he read
aloud: "Olai Vikssen Morstad. Born 14th April, 1886, Entered into
Eternal Rest, 9th March 1971. 84 Years 10 Months 24 Days!"

"Well, it ought to be 23 days, shouldn't it?" Vonnie shouted.

"Oh, Mom, it doesn't matter," the son called LeRoy said.

"Oh doesn't it! Well, people will just sit through the services,
you know what people are, and they'll count that up and they'll see
just as sure as anything someone didn't add straight. There'll be
talk."

"Come on, Mama," Mervin said. "Here's your coat . . . hat."
Harriet found and gave him Vonnie's black bag, her gloves.
"Come on, Mama," Mervin said, helping her. "They've got a real
nice dinner down at the church—and Corrine's are all there already
and they want to visit with you. And Mahlin's—all except Virgil,
he's away at school yet—" And gently he went on, listing the various relations who had come for the old man's funeral, and now
were being served a hot luncheon by one of the church circles. The
big men followed poor Vonnie out of the room—Mervin taking
her arm in the doorway. LeRoy hung back a minute and said civil-
ly, "I know what you done for our Ma, Mrs. White. All these years.
She wouldn't get by near as good without you being so good to stay
by. So thank you then!" A final view of his huge blushing face.

"Oh, Larry!" Harriet cried. "It's so good to see you!" For her son
was there: all that while, he'd been waiting in that crowded room,
quietly sitting on the edge of her bed near the far wall, glancing
through her books.

They hovered a moment, hugging each other, in the middle of

the room; "Mama," he said delighted, like a boy: "Look what I brought!"

There was a huge bundle of what looked like used clothing on her bed.

"You can hold it if you're good!" Larry laughed. He picked up the clumsy package, unwinding some of the clothes.

Harriet darted over without a word. Trembling, she undid the rest of some old padded jacket the baby was wrapped in, loosened his knit blanket—not without noticing through her tears, though, that it was one she had knitted. She carried Christopher to her rocking chair, and sat down. For a moment baby and great-grandmother made tiny struggles to get sorted. Harriet had to get her good foot, the left, which never gave her trouble even recently, onto the ground, to use for pushing to make the chair rock. The baby had to move his tiny shoulders as though scratching an itch, but in actuality, finding where and how this set of arms would hold him. He didn't pay much attention to what he saw out of his eyes: he saw only the dull whitish light off the snow, smeary and without warmth. What he felt in his shoulders, behind the small of his back, under his knees, was the very soul of whoever was holding him; it streamed into the baby from all those places. The baby stilled, paying attention to it, deciding, using shoulder blades, backbone, and legs to make the decision whether or not the energy entering was safe and good. Everything now told him it was, so in the next second, he let each part of his body loosen into those hands, and let his feet be propped on that lap, then let his chest be lifted and pressed to that breast and shoulder—his colorless rather inexpressive eyes went slatted half-shut. He made a little offering of his own; he let his cheek lean on that old, trustworthy cheek, and then, with a final wiggle, he gave himself up to being held. All she ever said to him was, "Christopher, precious!" but that was nothing to him—that was just noise.

Larry had stood up and gone over to the doorway; someone was conferring with him. He returned with a tray with two cups of coffee on it, and a plate with some white cake with inevitable Wilderness Cherry filling on it. "That was your head nurse—Mrs. Siegert, isn't it?" he asked, proudly keeping track of the Home staff.

He sat down on Vonnie's rocking chair, with the tray; he shoved Vonnie's Bible over. The lace bureau cloth immediately caught in one corner of it and wrinkled up, and the program for Ole Morstad's funeral, a paper rabbit candy basket, and a tube of Chap Stick fell on the floor.

Larry, sipping his coffee, told his day's news. It hadn't been a bad drive out from Edina, although Evelyn had sworn he would run into snow. One hundred and fifty miles with very few icy patches this time—not like last year at this time! "Met some of your menfolk here, in the hallway, on the way up," he added conversationally. "I told them who I was and they said, 'Oh sure, we know your mother! She's a real alert, real nice lady!'"

"I'm a regular Miss Jacob Lutheran Home!" Harriet said.

They both laughed, and he told her Evelyn sent her love. He told her about bringing Janice, his oldest son's wife, out to see her folks in Boyd, and how he begged the baby away from her on condition he wrap him up well.

"What farm business did you come about?" Harriet said, meaning to ask intelligent questions, although in truth she was only holding the baby.

"Oh that—" Larry said, frowning. "Before I get to that, there's something we've been over before, Mother, and I want to say it all again."

"Yes—all right!" She laughed at him ironically, mainly because it felt so marvelous holding the baby. His little eyes were half open, but she held him so close, up to her cheek, that the eye against her cheek was of course out of focus, and therefore only a dark blur: she thought, I shall never forget that look of a baby's eye when you hold him too close to see—the dark, blurry, soft fur-bunch of his eye!

"You know that Evelyn and I have plenty of room, Mama. We want you, Mama. This is O.K."—he gave a kind of wave at the tray of Marge Larson's birthday cake and Vonnie's mirror—"but, Mama, we want something different for you."

"You're right," Harriet said gently, "we *have* been over this before. You know how touched I am you feel that way, Larry. You and Evelyn."

She imagined again their house in Edina. It was one of a Cape Cod Development—white, but with the green-black shutters hung behind, rather than hinged on top of, the outside woodwork, and therefore straightaway visibly fake. But they had some marvelous rooms in it—a kind of library with a woodburning fireplace and a Viss rug with a light blue pattern, and the dining room. The other rooms had somehow soaked up the builder's ideas, and they all seemed to wail, Edina! Help! Evelyn had done what she could, but the built-in hi-fi cabinet in its fake Early American paneling suffocated the walls.

This wasn't why Harriet didn't go to live with them, but she conjured up the picture anyway.

"I know perfectly well you moved in here because that was the right thing for Dad," Larry was saying. "That was *then,* Mama. True, he would have been a burden on us—you never said that, but we knew that's what you thought. Anyway it's all different now, and I want you to reconsider. Very carefully."

"There's still your dad to think of, you know," Harriet remarked.

Larry put down his cake. "I don't know if that's true or not," he said. "I mean I don't know if that's the right thinking for you or us to be doing at all. I can't think it would make any difference—and meantime I've got a mother 150 miles away from me that I'd like to have living with me if you don't mind." He spoke a little feverishly—which Harriet understood as slight insincerity on his part.

"I don't know how to thank you," she said. She squinted hard into the baby's sleeping shoulders. His wooly sweater and the upper lip of his blanket she felt clearly on her eyelids. "I expect I could thank you by knitting baby blanket number 234 for Christopher here?"

They both laughed a little, but Larry let the laugh fall and quickly took up his point again. "And Evelyn feels the same way, too, Mama."

Harriet was thinking as fast as she could. She had to think: why was Larry feverish? He must be talking excitedly because he didn't really feel so enthusiastic about her moving in with them as he wished to show. Or, that he felt enthusiastic about it now, but that the offer really—very deep within him—was good only so long as his mother was sprightly, alert, a little witty, and so forth. And that he was not giving her the profoundly felt invitation—which would be an invitation to live with him and Evelyn when she might be incontinent, irritable, afraid, or even demented. And perhaps she, like Einar, would have a bad stroke.

As Harriet went through this in her mind, being as systematic about it as she could, she felt this last was the real explanation of Larry's nervousness. It reassured her in her refusal to live with them: even if she should choose not to consider Einar, and went to her son, she would still have to adjust to the Home later—to this one or to an unfamiliar one.

Having thought this through to the end, she gained her poise. She said kindly, "I know Evelyn feels that way. And I know you do, too—both of you—well, you're marvelous children. I'm going to stay put, I think, though. You know I thank you very much."

"Well, there's another reason, Mama," Larry said.

Harriet looked up, still feeling the new sense of control from having thought through the whole thing.

"You see, Mama, I've actually sold the farm. That's one reason I am out here this weekend."

She felt damaged. This piece of news was like an actual danger to her body. The trouble with being at the end of life, Harriet thought, was that body and mind get too close together: that is, when the mind takes a blow—such as from Larry's selling the farm—the body takes the blow as well. You feel the thing physically. Other times, she had noticed it worked in reverse. When she had originally tripped over Orrin Bjorning's bird-feeding station he left on the floor of the crafts room—a good five years ago now—not only had she hurt her right ankle and toe, but she had felt a kind of damage to her soul. Tears of hurt feelings had come, she remembered. Senility, she suspected, arrived the day you forgot to laugh at these incidents.

Rapidly she now went over Larry's actual words. If he hadn't literally sold the farm, she might convince him not to. But she thought she could still hear his voice saying he had already done it.

He hadn't asked her. She didn't expect to be begged for advice, but it would have been lovely, really lovely, if he had let her in on the various stages of the dealing. He could have told her, I'm beginning to consider offers on the farm, Mama. Or, Well, Mama, two of the buyer prospects look pretty good.

No doubt he had sensed that she would try to talk him out of it! In any case, she gathered herself carefully, meaning to have nothing of the wounded about her.

"You ought to sell the farm, my dear," she said smoothly. "You can't manage a piece of real estate properly unless you're right there, available, when things come up—and goodness knows, it doesn't look as if you and Evelyn are ever going to farm—and certainly Janice and Bob aren't moving in that direction. And I can't really think any of you would want to *retire* to the farm. No, that was probably a good thing!"

Larry gave her a sharp look but she gave away nothing—he surely saw only half old-woman-being-sensible, half great-grandmother-holding-the-baby.

"I don't want you to get around me this time, Mama," Larry said. "I want you to come live with us. We have all that room now. And time. And there'd be congenial people for you to meet. We're not country club people you know! Look, Mama—you've spent your whole life out here!"

The loudspeaker made its electric whine, and the pastor's hoarse, nasal voice came on with the table prayer. *"I Jesu navn går vi til bords, å spise og drikke på ditt ord. . . ."* It was dinner time at the Home—and the only sound on the second floor was the soft rub of nurses' shoes, as they moved about their duties.

"Let's go to lunch!" Larry said, standing. "Which one of the marvelous French restaurants of Jacob, Minnesota, shall we take in today? McGregor's Cafe or the Royal?"

"Neither for me," Harriet said. "Give me ten more minutes, dear—and then you go because I've got to go to that funeral this afternoon—and I just had cake and coffee. I don't want more now."

On a scaffold outside, Arne was manhandling a large screen frame. Apparently he had decided to start with the taking down of the storm windows after all. Both Harriet and Larry watched him a moment, in the way people who have done any job many times can't help pausing to watch someone else tackle it. They nearly felt the weight in their hands of the storm window coming off—they knew which snapholders had been loosened first; they knew the instant the weight of the glass and wood dropped into the vault of Arne's palm.

"You don't feel bad about the farm then?" Larry said, still looking out the window. Arne's shadow kept sliding back and forth in the room.

"No, dear. It was a good idea. Probably, you should have done it ages ago."

"You used to like it when we drove out there and checked out the old place," he said. "You'll miss that."

"Nonsense. There're hundreds of places I enjoy driving past."

"If you won't come to lunch, Mama, I've got to take that baby back to his mother, I'm afraid. You're sure you won't come?"

Christopher had wet through his clothing a little; his blanketed bottom was moist and warm, but Harriet, whose arm had ached the past half hour, couldn't bear to part with him. This moist, hot weight seemed like a part of her—she dreaded handing him over. She dreaded it. Yet, a minute later, when Larry carefully reached down, she managed a social smile up. Suddenly her breast and lap were cool. She felt abominable, never to nurse or hold a baby again. Her heart turned really black; she felt her whole body was like a cold andiron.

Larry promised to write, to repeat the invitation. They kissed and he left, saying he'd go see Dad on the way out.

Harriet waited until from down the hall she heard the elevator doors open, close, then she hurried out herself.

"Oh, *ja!* there she goes!" cried Helmstetter, sitting in his usual place at the landing. So everyone was up from dinner already.

Now there were four other men taking up all the chairs there, or she'd have joined him. They all looked especially fragile and pale because they had now put on their good suits; the corrugated necks were so thin, they touched their white collars only at the ribby cords. They were all ready for the funeral.

The two candy-stripers were approaching the elevators from the new wing; glasses and pitcher tinkled like little bells on their cart.

"Hullo, Mrs. White!" they both said.

"Hello—DeAnn . . . Mary."

"Oh my," the one called DeAnn said, cocking her head at the men sitting about, "aren't we dressed up all fine and nice! Everybody looking so nice!"

"They're going to a funeral," cried the other candy-striper.

DeAnn swung the light cart about. Mary had to step back, so it could enter the elevator when the doors opened. "Well they all look real nice," DeAnn sang. She pointed her arm at full-length to press the elevator button, and turned her firmly permanented head to the men. "Mr. Morstad was a real fine man," she sang to them. "And he looked real nice, too, for the services."

"I didn't think he did!" said Mary in a low tone to Harriet, dodging close to make room for the head nurse, Mrs. Siegert, who came up to wait beside them. Looking younger than 14 and very exposed, Mary seemed to gather her bravery and she blurted out, "I didn't think he looked very nice! He looked so tiny and brown and . . ." Her voice faded in terror, for the head nurse, as well as DeAnn, who no doubt despised her, and the four old men in the lounge chairs, now were staring at her.

"And dead," Harriet said, helping. "I agree. But then, the funeral had to be the fourth day instead of the third so the relatives could get here—that's why." Harriet brought out her best, sensible tone: "I remember on the first day he looked rather like himself—only asleep. The second day he began to look diminished, somehow. I remember thinking, that face wants to *leave.* The face is begging us to let it go—like a guest on the porch trying to get away from an

officious host. .... Then, yesterday, I remember—I happened into
the chapel coming from my walk, and he looked simply like a dead
man—he had lost all distinction. It wasn't that he wasn't preserved
or anything like that—but just that he had got generalized—he had
become a sampling of death."

The candy-striper's hands came together. "Oh yes!" she cried.
"Yes—exactly—that's how he was!" Still the elevator hadn't come
down. The light showed it was on three, and they could hear metal
scraping and men drawling instructions on the floor above.

The young candy-striper whispered, leaning over the cart toward Harriet, "I even noticed a tear under his eyelashes, Mrs.
White."

"Oh for goodness' sakes!" the head nurse snapped.

"That happens," Harriet said. "I know what that racket is," she
said to Mrs. Siegert. "I bet Arne's stuffing storm windows into that
elevator—"

They had still to wait, half-listening to the scraping noises upstairs as something was fitted into or out of the elevator.

"You girls hold back with that cart," Mrs. Siegert said, when the
elevator came. "Let Mrs. White get in first." But when the tall
metal doors had slid open, no one could get in, for the elevator was
full of men and a stretcher—Arne, now in his good dress suit, and
Mr. Solstad, the mortician, both men standing soldierly beside a
stretcher cart. The significant mounds and hollows under the
white sheet told the mind *A body is lying there*, but such an obser-
vation was only academic. Harriet couldn't seriously believe in a
human being under there. "We'll be done with the elevator in a
moment," Arne said. The doors closed again. Harriet, Mrs. Siegert,
and DeAnn watched the first floor light come on, and they all had
to listen to the elevator door springs downstairs, being struck open
twice. Harriet unwillingly imagined the body on its tray being
nudged and guided out.

Harriet and Mrs. Siegert walked down the third floor new wing.
The infirmary rooms ran along the north side, so they were walking along in direct light from the tall windows facing south. In the
middle of the corridor Ardyce, a very, very old person who had
been incontinent for over a year, stood urinating on the rubber
runner. Feeling the hot liquid course over her great ankles, she had
begun to cry. Her bony, caving body gave this shriek like some
poor sort of violin.

Mrs. Siegert was not an easily likable nurse, but she had her strong side; swiftly she got to Ardyce and had the limp elbow and said, "Don't cry, honey—I'll take you. We'll get cleaned up OK—don't cry"; they wobbled together to the old woman's room.

Two younger nurses were guiding a white-curtained screen out of number 307 on little metal wheels. "Oh . . . it was Mr. Kjerle?" Harriet asked.

One of the nurses bent to wipe up the urine from the corrugated rubber mat, and in a moment all was quiet again. Only mysterious breathing came from some room or another, and a cough like small twigs rubbing from some other room.

Harriet put her head into 307. She had meant to do whatever it is we intend in a place where someone has just died. She meant to give some honor or to wish him luck flying off the earth; she meant to help to lift him far off the curvature of the earth by evening. She wasn't clear about it but she felt somehow obligated. She crept into the room, if only to sense his possible presence. In any case, Harriet had expected the room to be empty. Everyone knew Mr. Kjerle's relatives never came to visit—only a retired piano teacher from two miles west of Jacob used to stop in sometimes. The piano teacher's visits weren't much. He really only prowled aimlessly about the infirmary room, not really visiting the old man, at least not keeping up a conversation. Whenever Harriet was up on the infirmary floor, he would waylay her, talk to her eagerly; sometimes, leaning in the doorway of 307, he would tell her it was cruel the way some of the residents never got any visitors.

Harriet was brought up short to see a woman sitting at the bare little desk under the window. She sat so still, and wrote with such concentration, that in the indifferent northern light, she looked positively spooky. She wore an elegant knit dress of dark lavender—for a second Harriet felt pleased, as if at a glimpse of the *grand monde*. Harriet received three impressions in rapid order: first, that this elegant figure writing was the spirit of the dead man; second, that it was some beautiful creature of society set here like a statue, just to give pleasure, and third—and she smiled with simple happiness at this—that it was the doctor.

Dr. Iversen didn't wear her medical jacket; like the other two doctors in Jacob, she avoided looking like a physician when she went to the Home. If you carried a medical bag, the old people snatched at you, telling of new sets of aches or about old prescriptions that didn't help anymore. Right now she had been called to the Home to "pronounce," that is, to legalize, a death. She had been sitting quietly, therefore, making out the certification.

"Hullo," she said courteously, as she saw a resident pause in the doorway. Then, with the instant calculation, the mental sorting of people that she exercised every day in her job, she added, "Mrs. White. Hullo, Mrs. White."

"How are you?" Harriet said, coming in, shyly. "I'm sorry, I didn't know anyone was in here."

"No, of course not," the doctor said. She had not quite finished, but without showing any haste, she quickly picked up the sheets, placing the printed side that read Minnesota Department of Health, Section of Vital Statistics, inward, against her hip. She rose. "How is that painful foot, anyway?" she asked.

"It isn't very painful," Harriet told her, gratified to be asked. "When it is, I take those gigantic tablets of yours anyway, and can't tell left foot from right!"

"Most of them," the doctor said, "wouldn't admit that a prescription ever did any good. I wouldn't dare ask how their foot is."

"By most of them I gather you mean most *old* people." Harriet laughed. "Don't talk so quickly! I shall be like that someday—and so will you. In fact, it's too bad you're so much younger—we could sit in our rocking chairs and tell each other what ached, and neither one of us would pay the slightest bit of attention to the other one. In fact, maybe you'll be worse. You'll be tired of listening to other people complain."

"No change, I suppose?" the doctor inquired, nodding toward the wall between the room they were in, number 307, and the next, 308.

"I haven't been in today—I'm just going now," Harriet said.

"It is hard, isn't it?"

"Yes—and I feel so sorry for him," Harriet added, not having planned to say anything like that.

Room 308, like 307, faced north, the cold light seeming simply to stand outside. There was the same little window desk, whose purpose was simply to be a piece of furniture for a sickroom. There was a high bureau, on which stood favors sent up from the public school children. At Christmas there had been paper reindeer with sleighs made of egg carton sections. Now there was an Easter bunny, stapled to a bit of egg carton, in which one or two of the hard candies that must have filled it remained. Harriet supposed the staff took a candy now and then, just as they gradually were taking the bureau space. In the top drawer were the clothes Einar had worn when they brought him up. But in the other drawers were odds and ends, a few more added right along, a small plastic bag of curlers, some lip moisturizing cream, two magazines read by the candy-striper who spoon-fed patients, half a box of tissues. More and more that had nothing to do with Einar seemed to sift into the room; his small influence, like a little scattering of pebbles, was being buried lightly under other influences.

Harriet spent a second by the desk, her eyes on the fields, plowed black, and to the north the semis moving like little blocks on U.S. 75. Then she straightened and went back over to the bed.

"Hello, dear," she said. She pulled the white-painted rocker over and sat down to talk to him. On the good days he gave a sound, as well as he could, to recognize her; on the other days, no particular sign. Today—nothing; so she settled to talk to him. "A little news for you, Einar," she said. "Larry's selling the farm— probably a very good idea," she went on. "And considering the condition of the buildings, he did very well I think. There's no doubt that was the right idea—selling the farm."

She paused. She pulled herself together again. "I gave him the go-ahead on that. . . ." She was trying to remember other things to tell; she remembered in the crook of her elbow, with the palm of her hand, the feeling of Christopher in her arms, but the memory was still too personal. In fact, it was not yet a memory, but still part of herself and therefore couldn't be told. "I gave another speech this morning," she went on cheerfully. "Anyway"—she smiled— "the speech went off all right. About the only other news is I've fairly well planned little Christopher's sweater now, so I'll start the knitting of it soon. Oh yes—and the men said to give you their best. That Helmstetter whose first name I never can remember— and Kermit—they both said to greet you. They were telling me about television. They don't watch 'Edge of Night' anymore, they said. They watch something called 'Splendor of Our Days.' It sounds dumber than the other one, but I expect if you kept track of it all the time, it would begin to seem real—you'd begin to care what happened to those people. . . . But those television characters don't seem like real people at all—and you know, they never show *where* the people are—they're always in a room somewhere—you never see a real place that counts, like a farm or anything like it— it's as if none of them had any place to belong to. Did I tell you, Larry sold the farm, Einar? Yes—very good idea, too!" She talked to him some more, and then rose saying, "I'll be back at five again to help you with your dinner, dear," and she went out.

She had spoken truthfully to the doctor in saying her right foot was not painful. When she finally got outside with her hat and scarf and gloves, she swung along well, and drew deep breaths of the cold, burdened air. It definitely was going to snow. She lightly dropped down the hill to the traffic circle, noticing all the cars and the hearse parked in the church lot. She turned west on 11th Street and was still moving freshly and gladly when she came to U.S. 75, with the closed Dairy Queen building and Waltham's Flower Shoppe.

When she turned north, on the right-hand shoulder of the highway, the wind struck her forehead. It wasn't bitter, but it was colder than she had hoped for. She turned away from it, long enough to pull her scarf up about her neck better, and now the buildings of the town, even the hasty gimcrackery of the Dairy Queen, looked protective and familiar. Well, I don't have to walk all the way to the farm on the ugliest day of spring, she told herself wryly, but she turned into the wind again, bending her head. Under her feet the dozens of pebbles on the road's shoulder underfoot looked shrunken and abandoned. She tried to set up her walking motion into a kind of automation, the way she and Einar and Larry had done for years and years when they were tired from the farmwork. At first you grew tired, then you grew so tired you felt you might cry, and then, by not feeling any pity for any part of your body, by not weakening those parts, that is, with pity, you actually exacted from them more character; once the ankles, back, shoulders, wrists, learnt to expect no mercy of you, they began to work as if automated. Then you weren't exhausted anymore, and you could sift fertilizers, or lift alfalfa, or shovel to an auger for hours and hours, until, with their headlights glowing like tiny search beams, coming out of the fields as if out of the sky itself, the tractors came home with the men who had been hired—and everyone could quit. Thus the tiredness could be held back until you all leaned over the salmon hot dish, and reached for the bread.

Harriet did the same thing now, looking up only once really— taking in a field of corn that someone hadn't gotten plowed, or even disked down at all. It'd do it good to snow a little, she thought of the scenery critically. So she was delighted like a child when the first flakes blew at her, around three-thirty.

It took her another two hours to get to Haglund's Crossroads, and a half hour to the farm from there. This last half hour was the

township road running east, however, so the steady snow, that had
been hurting her forehead, now struck only her left cheek, and she
took her second wind cheerfully. When she reached the corner of
her farm, she felt surprised: her old land, not ten feet from her now,
across the ditch past the telephone company marker, looked just
like all the fields she had been walking past. When she had sat on
the porch in the hot evenings, all the dozens of years she and Einar
had had the place, she certainly never would have thought those
particular sights—Elsie Johnson's barn with the louver-window
towers, Vogel's run, the Streges' line of cottonwoods to the south—
would lose their distinction. When Larry had taken her out for
rides, she always knew the place. Yet now, this late afternoon, she
felt no particular recognition.

"Well, but the house will make the difference—when I can see
the house," she said. Because the driveway lay another quarter of a
mile to the east, she decided to cut across the plowing instead. She
paused and then went down into the ditch, some pebbles falling
into her boots, and then slowly up, and began working along the
headlands of the field. Her forehead was tight and silky now with
cold, and the skin gave an unpleasant sensation of not being close
to her head. Harriet moved carefully, not just because she was exhausted, but because it was borne in on her that she was a very old
woman and she would make a fool of herself if she fainted out here
in the middle of nowhere, with night coming on.

The plowing was coarse, and from her height—as she imagined
herself an airplane passing over it—it became a chain of harsh,
tumbled mountains, with peaks turning floury, but the smooth
sides, scoured by the shares, still gleaming black. At last the farmhouse, or at least some dark, square, blessedly man-made shape,
stood out 100 yards ahead. Its lightless windows, broken, and tum-
bledown porch seemed friendly and very memorable. It had been a
marvelous idea to come—marvelous!

Harriet's fingers, particularly on the right hand, were starting to
freeze, but she put them in her coat pocket and went forward quickly. She also planned ahead, using her common sense: she would
stay in the house or around it, but not for more than half an hour.
She wasn't a fool; it would be difficult to explain why she'd come,
but if she left soon and got home, she might even not be missed.

The rough plowing ended; she stepped into the spineless pigeon
grass, and emptied her boot. The snow stopped, but enough was
down so the farmyard, with the L-shaped old house on it, rose a
pale, glowing mound. Harriet went happily up.

The front door was half-ruined and stood open. She decided that it would be depressing inside the house so she sat down gratefully on the edge of the porch, feeling sorry for its beautifully milled railing posts wrecked and lying in the snow. She crossed her hands in her lap—a trick she had had all her life—in order to think deliberately, and get things right.

Immediately her mind and body seemed to have opposing wishes. Her mind wanted to go over favorite memories—it wanted to swoon, to graze, to be languid, and to rove over things that are delicious, such as her old loves. Her own mother and father, for example, whom she visualized dancing in their club, or drinking with faces yellow from the firelight at home. The mind wanted to go over how she loved them although she had despised their shallow, rich, greedy life; how much she loved her parents and would like to know what they were thinking now . . . It wasn't a new line of thought but her mind wanted so very much to go over it again. But her body, or her soul, whichever it was, was thoroughly excited and seemed to be urging, something very strange is about to happen! It was alerted like an animal—it refused to let her dream along the old intelligent reflections—it wanted to get the scent of something, it seemed to send fingers out beyond the broken porch. Oh—she thought, holding these two parts as well as she could—it is definitely something spiritual, something about to happen! And not from inside me! All these years I assumed it was all inside me—but apparently it isn't!—and I am afraid! In any case, it was in the outer circle of darkness now, rising over the Haglund Road maybe; anyway it lay outside the farm, and was lifting and falling, coming in closer, without any excitement of its own, simply waiting, not crouching nor threatening—something calm, but mortally large. She needed to invite it, Harriet felt, if it was to come in any closer.

Then a third thing happened: headlights were moving along the snowy road to the south, going east the way Harriet had come, and then going past the place where she had turned up through the field. Now the invisible car presented its red taillights for a moment but then, in the next, the headlights swung left and were quartering on Harriet. So they knew she was gone and had figured she might do just this—walk up here; and they were coming, to save her from the cold and dark. Her hand, particularly the fingers, hurt enough; she nearly leapt forward gratefully.

Wait a moment, she thought, sensibly: there are three different

things I can do. I can still run behind the house—it isn't too late—
they would call about a little here and there, but they wouldn't
think of the old chickenhouse we had used for lawn mowers.
Then, whatever that part of her was that wanted to invite the huge
mortal thing outside, would have a little more time to do it in. But
no, Harriet thought, as intelligently as she could, they would see
her footsteps in the snow and she would be tracked like an animal,
and she would never recover her pride—not ever, after that. Now
the headlights were fully turned in her direction, and as soon as the
car tipped up to make the rise, the lights would flood over her, as
the lights of all their visitors always had, blinding anyone on the
porch. It was going to be unpleasant, whatever happened. She
tried very hard to think of some little speech to give that would not
let them find her old and out of her wits—something to pass it off
lightly—but how? For she didn't feel she had any light touch at the
moment at all: more and more, her soul was being engaged by the
gigantic, mortal thing waiting in its wide arc outside. One minute
it seemed to offer to go away, and leave her with her ordinary life in
her hands again. This she couldn't bear, not now that she'd once
seen it. She had a taste for it now. The next minute, however, she
found she was still unready, too frightened by far, and she would
agree to marry any sort of dullness rather than to join whatever
that was. She couldn't toss off anything with a laugh now. If she
herself were so deadly serious, how could she hope to make whoever was driving up in this car take the whole thing lightly?

Now the headlights were brilliant on her, so she had to look
down at the wrecked railing and posts, that lay like a ladder thrown
down in the snow. The headlights came no closer: the car must
have stopped, and she heard the incredible confidence of an American automobile engine idling in neutral. Doors clicked open and
shut—men were tramping in the darkness behind the headlights—
someone in a low tone could be heard saying, "It's her all right!"
Another voice—"You all wait. I'll go up!" Then a gigantic black
profile of someone came at her, shielding her from the beams.

"Hi, Mama," the man said.

In a flash Harriet was angry at this grown Larry—a shallow
thing he seemed, no matter that he was her son, no matter he was
being dear and dignified and not talking at her, helping her step
over the smashed banister in the snow. But she thought, how different he is from the baby he was, with the dark, blurry eyes so close
to her face, for now he was only a grown son—predictable, and
wrapped around with his health and sense.

Other people sat in the car. As Harriet got into the front seat, she saw all their faces in the light from the car's ceiling—Arne, it was; Larry; Siegert, the head nurse; some other nurse she had seen but didn't know—and she felt comforted, partly, by this lighted little circle. Outside the car, in a much wider circle, the mortal presence still wafted lightly. Harriet felt very definitely that it was offering to lap forward toward her again. She felt she could rally it and offer to go out with it, like something bobbing on lumpy, stale seawater in the darkness; she felt it wouldn't take her quickly. It would lap forward and receive her, but for a while it would let her look back to the tiny car, with the tiny circle of human beings. But they were all she knew, so she fled into the front seat, and let herself be walled up with Arne's shoulder on one side, moving as he went into reverse, and Larry's great shoulder on the other side. And from the back seat came low, special voices—the nurses talking to each other professionally. Harriet hoped she had not lost individuality from their point of view: now she was a woman who wandered off from the Home and had to be brought back at a good deal of inconvenience, and on such a busy day. She must be very careful to be light and sociable. "So good of you all," she murmured. "It was very cold."

She was very grateful for losing the sensation of God being close— or perhaps she had made up in her mind the whole impression of something in the darkness. In any case it didn't matter. She hadn't the slightest curiosity to think it over, for something much worse occupied her. Squeezed between these kind men, with the car heater blowing hot breath into her face, and with her eyes full of dancing needles and blue tiny fires on the dashboard, she was sharply aware that she wasn't safe with these protectors. Her hand was in great pain now, from the freezing: but suppose *all* of her were in pain, and suppose death did come, and not some death she chose to conjure up and call upon, but plainly death himself, the real one— she would flash down like silk between these men, past the glittering dashboard, without leaving the slightest impression, the way the pebbles in the road were blown off by the speeding car. I'm simply not going to be able to do anything about it, she thought with surprise.

They were driving rapidly down the Haglund Road—she felt the millions of pebbles of gravel that had always lain there, unwrapped, which no one pays any attention to, all the millions of things that lie about unbound to the millions of other things. With a tremendous burst of humility and joy Harriet thought:

what a tremendous lot I have failed to think through! Yet I always thought I thought through things so well!

From a mile and a half north, the Jacob Lutheran Home suddenly stood up, with its three stories of lighted windows. It was difficult to visualize the shuffling heels moving about near bureaus, or to believe in the cartful of magazines parked idle for the night in the coffee room. The Home looked at least like a mighty office complex where far-reaching decisions are made that affect common people without their even knowing it. It was difficult to believe in Einar up there, lying lightly gowned in white, scarcely touching, like a bit of string, as he had lain for fourteen months. Harriet thought, And I shall lie up there, too, and from month to month, because I will no doubt get less amusing and I will get more frightened, there will be fewer and fewer visitors, even this huge man next to me, Larry, my son, will come much less often, and perhaps my death will rock forward and backward on its heels waiting a long time, and I shall be so diminished by the time it comes even the staff won't feel anything personal. There will be none of the old recognition . . .

They were approaching the confident little town. Harriet was very surprised to find that she hadn't spent eighty-two years in love with all there is, with tiny things like pebbles, which were in some strange way her equal; pebbles were her equal; she was astounded she had missed it! Now she needed every possible second, even if it were to be spent in a daze. How could she ever have said, "It is cruel that so-and-so's life drags on like this!" or, "It is a blessing that death came to so-and-so!" Or, "I certainly hope I shall go quickly when I go"—as if it were a question of being fastidious.

The heat of the car did not help her frozen hand. The pain was frightful—but her thoughts seemed so much more frightful to her that she deliberately gave in to the pain. From the back seat came kind voices: "Soon there, Harriet . . ." and "You're not the only one to go out walking, you know," and "We all do it, Harriet . . ." And in the front seat, her son's shoulder jerked a little next to hers and he stared ahead, silently, through the windshield.

When they were up in room 211, the doctor examined her fingers carefully. "We'll have you knitting again—it won't be long," she said. "She can have something to help her sleep," she said pointedly to the head nurse, who paused in the doorway.

Larry sat on Mrs. Ole Morstad's bed, with his knees spread, his hat thrown up on the pillow. He was turning over Harriet's alarm clock, and he looked very tense and bored. Harriet, too, felt very strained and bored.

"If you would *please* reconsider, Mama," Larry was saying— still asking her to go live with him. A second ago her heart had leapt—but only for a second. She would love to leave this fate! She would love to go to him! Again she imagined his house, the flowery rug with its wide edge of sky blue that looked like a cool, ancient summer all the time, and the marvelous tone of the Vivaldi on his record machine; Janice would come on weekends, perhaps, and bring the baby, and Harriet would rock with the baby, and look at all the woolen yellow flowers in the rug.

Larry was making the offer, but she heard a new apprehension in his voice. I am a very old woman apparently, she told herself, and I've wandered off in a snowstorm, but I'm not going to add this to my other sins. As she turned him down, she smiled quite genuinely, because the pill she'd been given was taking effect—her hand no longer hurt—and everything looked peaceful and color- less. From time to time, the upper echelon of the staff and residents looked in and greeted her—Marge Larson the therapist even stopped a moment, Kermit Steensen nodded from the hall—the candy- stripers had long since gone home or she knew Mary would have greeted her.

Tomorrow morning, word would have got around the whole community, and the simpler, the very aged, or the less acquainted people would take to hobbling by room number 211. They would want to have a look at someone who had stirred the community by getting a notion to go back home. From their flagged, lifeless ex- pressions it would be hard to understand that actually their hearts were rather aflutter with this Harriet White's doings—the way the hearts of young women feel roused, and unstable, and prescient, when the first of their friends is going to marry.

CAROL BLY's second collection of stories, *The Tomcat's Wife and Other Stories* (HarperCollins, 1991), won the Friends of American Writers Award. Five of her essays are included in *Eight Modern Essayists,* edited by William Smart (St. Martin's Press, 1990). She is also the author of *The Passionate, Accurate Story: Making Your Heart's Truth into Literature* (Milkweed Editions, 1990), the essay *Bad Government and Silly Literature* (Milkweed Editions, 1987), and the acclaimed book of essays *Letters from the Country* (Harper & Row, 1981). She co-authored *Soil and Survival: Land Stewardship and the Future of American Agriculture* with Joe and Nancy Paddock (Sierra Club Books, 1986).

Bly was the Benedict Distinguished Visiting Professor of English at Carleton College (Spring 1990). She teaches Ethics at the University of Minnesota; she is a frequent lecturer, a humanities consultant to the Land Stewardship Project, and serves on the Board of Directors of the Loft. She received an honorary doctoral degree from Northland College in 1992. Carol Bly lives in Sturgeon Lake and St. Paul, Minnesota.